THE FINE LINE

Book One

Between Worlds Series

TRACEE FORD

ISBN: 9780692413593

DEDICATION

This book is dedicated to all of the people who

stood behind me on this project, believing in its reality.

Special thanks to Eileen and Jeannie.

My son, David, for your

patience and encouragement.

Love you.

Very special thanks to the first editor of this book, Richard Sprigg.

CONTENTS

ACKNOWLEDGMENTS

This book was shaped over time, and I am grateful for the patience, understanding, and quiet support that made its completion possible. To those who offered encouragement, space, and steadiness along the way. Thank you for staying present while this story found its way to the page.

I also acknowledge the creative support and tools that assisted during revision and refinement, helping to clarify structure, continuity, and voice in the final stages of this manuscript. Any remaining imperfections are entirely my own.

1

Exhaustion tugged Robin's energy levels lower than when she had been interning two years ago with a local hospital. She'd grown accustomed to the graveyard shift. Now her job with the government, while lucrative, demanded a lot of her. It was difficult adjusting to the lack of sleep.

She had taken a position with the county's children's services division doing ongoing cases. Because of her outstanding work, she'd been offered a promotion to the intake assessment department. It paid slightly better, but as with everything in life, there were sacrifices. One of those happened to be carrying the on-call pager.

With the police by her side, Robin worked feverishly through the night to help a sibling group get settled into their new foster home. Even though she'd been out all night, she reported to work promptly at 8 a.m. By 4:30 p.m., she was back at her apartment, asleep in bed.

At 5:50 p.m., she woke to her cell phone alarm blaring. She hurriedly put on her softball uniform, grabbed her cleats, swept her long dark brown hair up into her ball cap, and darted out the door. When she pulled into the parking lot, the rest of the team was already waiting.

As they did every year, the agency had a softball league. Tonight, the local sheriff's department hosted the event. Spectators were out in full force, too.

Robin played outfield. After three innings, she ran to the dugout triumphantly with the ball in her mitt. The children's services team needed more runs. As she stepped up to the plate, she knew this was their chance to jump ahead. She smiled at the pitcher. She knew him well. Deputy Marvin Reed had stood by her side a few times since she'd started with the investigations department.

Marvin threw the pitch. The crack of the bat echoed as it struck the leather ball. Teammates cheered as Robin rounded first and second base. Suddenly, she felt her left ankle twist. Before she knew it, she tumbled to the ground. Members of both teams ran to her. Pain throbbed in her ankle as she grabbed it instinctively, pulling it close to her body.

Wendy Snyder, Robin's best friend and roommate, a sweet yet outspoken woman, knelt beside her. "You think it's broken?"

"It hurts pretty bad. It's a shame we're not playing the paramedics tonight," Robin answered. She still held tightly to her ankle, praying it was simply a sprain.

"You tripped on that rock," Wendy said as she pointed toward the culprit. "We need to get you to the E.R. to have it looked at."

After helping her up and getting Robin into the car, the drive to the hospital was quiet. Robin checked in. Thirty minutes came and went. Finally, Robin was called into triage, where she explained everything to the nurse.

After the initial consultation, Robin made her way back out to the waiting area for another thirty minutes. She eventually heard her name called from the open door. Wendy helped Robin to her feet, and she hobbled toward the door. As she passed through, pastel-colored curtains filled her vision. The sounds of the E.R. echoed in her ears.

"The doctor will be in to see you shortly," the nurse said. She then turned and left.

A sigh escaped Robin's lips. Irritated and sleep-deprived, she flopped back onto the gurney. Her brown eyes closed as she gave up her fight against intense exhaustion. It felt as if she'd slept for only a minute when she felt a warm hand on her forehead. She thought she was dreaming until she heard a man's voice, smooth and comforting. She also heard Wendy's whispers. Wendy told the doctor about the incident at the ball field as well as Robin's terrible night on call.

"Miss Hillard," the voice said softly, his hand still resting on her forehead. "Miss Hillard, can you wake up for me, please?"

Her eyes opened to see a man in a white lab coat. She estimated him to be about five foot ten. His beautiful brown eyes were full of comfort. His dark brown hair was a tussled mess, shaggy with the front swept to the side. His navy scrubs complemented his light complexion.

Robin still struggled to find consciousness. She heard his sneakers scuff the floor when he shifted his weight. He smiled when her eyes finally opened to meet his gaze. His face was gorgeous. He had a precisely cut goatee, and his smile made her blush. Her pulse sped as she took in all of his features.

"Miss Hillard, I'm Dr. Gregory. Your friend tells me that you fell at a softball game?"

His hand moved from her forehead to his pocket as he pulled out a penlight. He flashed it in her eyes. Squinting and still irritated, she sat up and groaned. Her body felt lifeless as her energy level continued plummeting. Even her speeding pulse didn't overcome the fatigue. She flopped back down.

"Are you in any pain right now?" he asked. "Head spinning? Anything like that? Have you eaten anything?"

"One question at a time, please," she answered with a smile. "Yes, I'm in some pain. Yes, my head is spinning. I've had no sleep. And no, I haven't eaten since lunch."

"Just relax. I'm going to take a look at your leg and ankle first, and then we might run some tests just to rule out other things, okay?"

"What other things?"

"Well, are you usually pretty steady on your feet? Is it normal for you to fall?"

"Well, I'm clumsy by nature," she said. "Sometimes I have two left feet, but I've never fallen like that. Like I said, I'm tired. And I'm also sure the large boulder in front of third base didn't help much."

Robin felt his fingers on her ankle. She winced from the pressure of his touch.

"Tender there, huh?"

She nodded and folded her hands neatly on her stomach.

"X-rays first, but I don't think you broke it. The swelling is minimal. You probably just twisted it."

"Okay."

"Blood work to rule out anything else, and you need to eat something, so I'll have the nurse bring in a sandwich after we draw blood. Just relax and we'll get you fixed right up," he said as his hand touched hers.

When he left, Wendy smiled. "He's hot."

Robin agreed, but changing the subject was safer. "How long was I out?" she asked curiously.

"Only about an hour. They're really busy tonight." Wendy paused. "Are you feeling okay?"

"I'm just really tired and hungry."

The phlebotomist came into the room and took blood as Wendy's cell phone rang. She left the room to take the call. Another nurse came in with a turkey sandwich from the cafeteria.

Wendy walked back in and sat down. "Well, Terri called, and he and Dalton ran your car back to the apartment," she began. "They said they hope you didn't break your ankle because they really need you to cover for them while they're on vacation. They said, 'If you're off sick, you can't be of any help to anyone.'"

"Oh, is that all they care about?"

"Jamaica is more important than your ankle," Wendy added.

The curtain slid open, and Dr. Gregory appeared with a wheelchair. Robin wasn't expecting him. In fact, she expected a longer wait and a nurse to show up.

"Ready to get a good dose of radiation?" he asked jokingly.

She smiled. She felt woozy as she sat up on the side of the gurney. Quickly, the doctor was by her side, helping her stand.

"I don't think you should put weight on it until we find out more. Put your arm around my neck and I'll help you," he said as he smiled at her. Again, their eyes collided.

She put her arm around his neck and felt his arm slide around her waist. She hopped into the wheelchair with his assistance.

"I'll have her back in no time," he said as he smiled at Wendy.

"Shouldn't a nurse be doing this?" Robin asked candidly as he wheeled her out.

"Well, we are swamped tonight, and I don't mind doing the dirty work sometimes," he said with a heartfelt smile.

The silence was thick as they maneuvered through the hospital hallways. The silence, however, didn't last long.

"So, you injured your ankle playing for your softball league? What team do you play for?"

"I work for children's services in the next county over. We have a league."

"What position do you play?"

"Outfield mostly."

"You any good?"

"I think so. But as you can tell, third base got the best of me tonight," she continued as she gestured toward her ankle.

He laughed. "You should probably be a little more careful next time."

Once safely delivered to the radiology department, Robin expected Dr. Gregory to leave, but he didn't. Instead, he stayed with her. She found it odd, but comforting. His voice reassured her.

As they talked, they discovered that they shared many things in common. The conversation was easy. Robin observed him closely. She'd been trained to mind her surroundings as well as body language.

One of the first things she noticed was the absence of a wedding band. There was no tan line either. He must have a girlfriend, she thought. Someone that charming couldn't be single.

He seemed confident but not arrogant. Personable and kind. It surprised her based on her past experiences with doctors. Still, despite how great he seemed, Robin's instinct to be suspicious clouded her thoughts.

After the X-ray, he wheeled her back to her cubicle and helped her onto the gurney. He left, pulling the curtain closed behind him. Strolling to the nurse's station, he saw his close friend and colleague, Avery Walters, signing a chart.

"That didn't take long," Avery said.

"X-ray wasn't that busy." Matt paused. "So, is it unethical for me to ask her out?"

Avery shook his head. "I don't think so. What are the chances you'll see her again in here? She's not going to be a regular patient. But why her? Why not the last two?"

"I can't really explain it. She's very likable. There's just something different about her."

"So, you don't think it has anything to do with sex? Or should I say, the lack thereof lately?"

"Seriously, Avery? You know me. I'm not like that." He looked over at Robin's curtain. "What if she thinks I'm some crazy stalker?"

"She probably will," Avery laughed.

"Thanks a lot," Matt replied, rolling his eyes. He glanced toward the next chart.

"How long has it been since you actually asked someone out on a date?" Avery asked.

Matt thought. "I can't even remember."

"And when was the last time you had sex with anyone other than yourself?" Avery teased.

Matt glared at him.

Back behind the curtain, Robin rested on the gurney. A thousand thoughts raced through her mind; many centered around Dr. Gregory. His smile. His eyes.

"Well, what did he say?" Wendy asked.

Robin jumped, startled. She collected herself and smiled. "We just talked."

"Honey, have you not noticed how beautiful that man is? If you haven't, then they need to check your pulse because you might just be dead."

"He is cute, isn't he?"

"Cute is an understatement, girl."

The curtain slid open. Matt stepped inside with a black X-ray film. He grinned, and once again, their eyes locked. He placed the film on the light board.

"Just as I suspected, your ankle is twisted. Your blood work is perfect. No fractures. I suggest you stay off the ankle for a day and take some pain relief. Keep it iced and elevated tomorrow, and you should be okay by Thursday for sure. You should be running the bases by next week. Drink lots of fluids. That helps with swelling."

Relief swept over her. "Good. No breaks. I can't afford to be off work very long."

"I want you to take tomorrow off, but after that you need to decide whether the pain is tolerable. If it still hurts, don't go to work. It's better to let yourself heal. Work will wait."

"Can you write me off, Dr. Gregory?"

"That's no problem. And please, call me Matt."

She smiled. "Matt."

"I'm going to wrap your ankle in a bandage just to be on the safe side. The less you move it, the better. You can take this off when you're sitting, but when you're up, moving around, or sleeping, keep it wrapped and put very little weight on it."

Robin watched him walk to a drawer and retrieve an ace bandage. He laid it beside her leg, then walked to a nearby closet and pulled out a pair of crutches, propping them against the wall.

"These are going to be your best friends for the next week."

She frowned.

He returned to the end of the gurney. As he wrapped her ankle, they made small talk. He had a careful touch Robin appreciated.

Wendy left the room to offer some privacy.

Matt grinned sweetly as he helped Robin stand with the crutches.

"Thanks, doctor... I mean, Matt."

He smirked. "Listen, you'll probably think I'm crazy, but I was wondering if maybe sometime, you'd like to go out for coffee."

"I don't drink coffee," Robin said with a vague smile.

"Oh." His gaze dropped.

"But I could go for a meal sometime," she added.

2

Robin met Matt for breakfast after his graveyard shift on Saturday. The café near the hospital made for a convenient spot. Robin preferred a public venue. It took the pressure off. By accepting his invitation, she trusted her instincts with high hopes. He seemed like an all-right guy. Still, her past kept her cautious.

Robin pushed open the door to the café and scanned the restaurant. The place seemed like a living organism with clattering dishes and the hum of voices. In the back, she spotted Matt sitting in a booth, stirring a cup of coffee. He waved and stood as she walked toward him.

Her heart pounded as anxiety heightened, but she remained outwardly calm. She wondered if she looked pretty enough or poised enough. Her insecurities wrapped around her body like chains. Once again, his smile put her at ease.

Her light-colored jeans, red graphic T-shirt, flip-flops, and her hair in a messy bun conveyed her true identity. No frills. Average height with a slender build, Robin was healthy and fit.

She slid into the seat across from Matt. Their eyes met. A glass of water was already waiting for her.

"I take it the ankle is better. No crutches," he said.

"No crutches. I'm still using the bandage, though."

She picked up the glass of water and took a drink. After setting it back on the table, she made eye contact with Matt again.

"Rough night?" she asked thoughtfully. He looked weary, but she also saw the spark of anticipation.

"Na. Nothing I'm not used to." He took a sip of his coffee. "Robin, I'm sorry if I seemed like such a freak the other night. I don't normally ask people out that I've just met."

She smiled, not believing a word he said.

"There's just something about you," he continued. "I can't explain it."

"Uh-huh." She chuckled and shook her head.

"No. Seriously. You think it's a line, but it's not."

"Really?" Robin sighed, not convinced. "Oh, come on. You're a doctor. All doctors have a God complex. Most of them think pretty highly of themselves."

"Give me some credit," he said. "You need to give me a chance before you start…"

"Judging you," she finished.

"Well, yeah." His smile never faded.

"So, tell me who you are really," she began. "I know we talked a little bit the other night, but how much can you really learn from being around someone for a few hours?"

He cleared his throat and sat up straighter, almost as if he were in an interview. He folded his hands around his cup of coffee and began.

"I'm thirty-six. I went to The Ohio State University School of Medicine. I got married too young and then got divorced much later than I should have. I guess that's because I'm too tolerant. I have a six-year-old daughter who comes to see me every other weekend and throughout the summer. I haven't dated much since my divorce because after my ex-wife and I split up, I started thinking that perhaps all women are evil."

He laughed. She laughed with him, acknowledging his attempt to lighten the mood.

"I really don't like working nights, but it's hard to imagine myself working any other shift. I've been on nights since med school. But I suppose the upside is that most of the good stuff happens at night. After all, that's how we met, right? If I weren't assigned to the night shift, this opportunity could have sailed right by." He smiled sincerely.

"I have an older brother," he continued, "and my dad died of cancer two years ago. My mom is still living and loves to visit me unannounced during the day when I'm trying to sleep." Again, they laughed.

"My brother and I are very close, but we didn't used to be." He took another sip and went on. "When my dad died, my brother and his wife moved to Middletown to be closer to my mom. It took my dad's dying for my brother and me to realize how much our mom needed us and how dumb we'd been. So we put our stupidity aside and realized how futile the rivalry had been.

"I live in an apartment here in Oxford. I can walk to work, which I like, because my truck is a gas hog. Ultimately, I want to move to the country someday."

"You don't seem like much of a country boy," she interjected playfully.

"Well, you just met me, and you act like you know me or something," he joked.

Robin felt the blood rush to her cheeks, and she covered her embarrassment with laughter.

"Seriously," he continued, "I want to be where it's quiet. I was raised in the city. I need a change of scenery. My dad owned a construction company and taught me everything, so I could probably build a house with my bare hands if I wanted to."

"Impressive," she said with a nod.

"Well, I'd need some help, of course," he said, grinning. "I love rock-n-roll, American history, and my daughter is the most important woman in my life. I couldn't ask for a better kid."

"That's a good summation," Robin said, amused.

"Okay, now it's your turn."

He lifted his coffee cup back to his perfectly shaped lips.

She took in a deep breath. With a quick exhale, she began. "I'm twenty-six. I was born in May, thus the reason for my middle name. I graduated from the University of Dayton. I was enrolled in an accelerated program in high school, which allowed me to get most of my general education credits out of the way before I even officially started undergrad. I went straight through the summers and graduated with my bachelor's in two years. Then I enrolled in Wright State's social work master's program. I interned at Miami Valley Hospital, and that really prepared me for my LISW."

"So, you're a Licensed Independent Social Worker? Nice."

She nodded and continued. "I sort of fell into the job with Children's Services. A friend of a friend of a friend recommended I apply. So I did."

"Where are you from?" he asked.

"I'm from the southern part of Ohio, but when I moved here to go to school, I liked the area so much I couldn't leave."

She took a drink of water and cleared her throat before continuing. "I've never been married. I have no children. I share an apartment with Wendy, the girl who brought me into the E.R."

"She seemed to genuinely care about you."

"We were roommates in college. We're like sisters. She majored in health sciences." Robin paused, then looked down at her water before looking back up again. "I think she works in your hospital. I'm surprised you don't know her."

The grimace on his face revealed his surprise.

"What's her last name?"

"Newton. Dr. Ewley hired her."

"That explains it."

She tilted her head, curious.

"She's on the staff payroll, yes," he said. "But Dr. Ewley is a private practice doctor. His staff isn't directly associated with the hospital. That's why I haven't seen her before. She probably works days. Our paths just never crossed."

"That makes sense," Robin said.

He looked down into his coffee and then back up at her. "I'm sorry. I keep interrupting you. Please continue. I'm not done interviewing you yet." He smiled wryly.

"Well," she began again, "I have a younger sister and an older brother. My mom, stepdad, and siblings still live in the southern part of the state. I love my friends from work, and I truly love what I do. And just for the record, I'm not like most twenty-six-year-olds. I know who I am, and I have a clear picture of what I want. And I knew I wanted you to ask me out when we met."

She amazed herself with her boldness.

Surprised and pleased, Matt beamed. "Really?"

Despite her uncertainty, she nodded confidently and smiled. "I thought you were very handsome and very sweet." She hesitated before continuing. "I'll admit that things felt weird at first. Then I listened to you talk and watched you. I knew you weren't just being polite. Your interactions with me seemed like they meant more."

"I'm not usually taken off guard," he said, "and I was afraid asking you out would scare you. I didn't want you to think I was some sort of creep. Like I said, I don't date much."

Robin leaned in toward Matt and rested her elbows on the table. Folding her hands, she studied him carefully. "From what I see, you have a beautiful soul. You have a great sense of humor. Personally, I believe if you cannot laugh at life, then it's hopeless."

He leaned in too.

"Interesting perspective," he said pleasantly. "Are you psychic? What if I am a freak who stalks women with sprained ankles?"

"I'm a pretty good judge of character." The conviction in her tone reassured him.

"I may be going out on a limb here," he said in a seductive tone, "but there's a concert two Saturdays from now. I happen to have that night off. I have two tickets, and I wondered if you might want to go with me."

"Who's playing?" she asked, still leaning in.

"It's just a local band," he shrugged. "It really doesn't matter who's playing because I like live music. My buddy and his girlfriend are going, too."

"I would love to go."

"Awesome. Awesome." He smiled, settling back in his seat. "I'll pick you up at six? It doesn't start until seven-thirty, but we're driving to Cincinnati, so it'll be about an hour and fifteen minutes if traffic is good."

"Sounds like a lot of fun. Would you like to come to my next softball game to make sure I don't fall and break something?" she asked playfully.

"I'd love to come. When is your next game?"

"We always play on Tuesday and Thursday nights. I'll give you directions. We're playing the local police department on Tuesday and that's always entertaining. They're power freaks."

"I will be there. I don't have to be at work until ten on Tuesday."

"Our games usually start at six and are over by eight, sometimes earlier."

"Can I take you out to a quick dinner afterward?" he asked sweetly.

"We usually go out as a group for burgers. Why don't you come with us?"

"Sounds great," he replied. "Can I chat with you online this week? Maybe call you? You can give me the directions to the field?"

"Absolutely," she answered.

Before they knew it, two hours had passed. The dark circles under Matt's eyes were more pronounced as exhaustion set in.

"I think we may need to depart for now," Robin suggested.

"I am pretty tired," Matt admitted reluctantly.

Before leaving the diner, they exchanged phone numbers, email addresses, and social media information. They said their goodbyes and went their separate ways.

That night, before Matt went to work, they chatted online. Over the coming days, they exchanged text messages and a few phone calls.

Robin enjoyed getting to know Matt. He was funny, and she loved listening to him laugh. She noticed he also had a serious side. He was winning her over quickly. Nevertheless, she remained cautiously optimistic.

Robin's genuine thoughtfulness attracted Matt. He was drawn to her beauty and intelligence. Most of all, he recognized her honesty and integrity.

3

Robin sat at the kitchen table, eating her cereal. The apartment was quiet. Wendy stayed with Terri at his apartment most of the time anyway. They had been together for several years. Terri had helped Robin get the job with the children's services agency.

He had a stocky build with brownish-red curly hair. He was good-hearted and charitable. He and Wendy were a perfect match. They were incredibly compatible and made one another very happy.

Wendy was biracial with beautiful blueish-green eyes. She was 5'8" and towered over Robin. Through good and bad, Wendy was a loyal friend. She was authoritative and confident. Robin envied her for that.

The front door slammed. Robin smiled with anticipation. She couldn't wait to share the exciting news about Matt.

Wendy walked into the kitchen. She grabbed a pastry from the cabinet and then opened the fridge for a protein shake. As she sat down across from Robin, she smiled. "Morning, sister," she said.

"Morning," Robin replied.

"What's up? I feel like I haven't talked to you in ages."

"All sorts of things are happening," Robin started.

"Well, girl, do tell! I'm sorry I haven't been around, but with Terri leaving on vacation, it's been a little crae-crae."

"I know." Robin nodded. "It's okay. You're a good girlfriend," she said sincerely. "So… Matthew Gregory. Have you heard anything about him?"

"That's the hunky E.R. doctor, right?" Wendy asked.

"Yes," she replied as her cheeks flushed pink.

"Wow. I didn't even put two and two together," Wendy said pensively.

"What do you mean?"

"I don't know him," she continued, "but I have heard of him. He used to be married to Sheryl Winston. She's some big shot in the neonatal unit. Their divorce was big news."

"I see."

"Sheryl is a lot older than Matt. She is not very popular at the hospital. Frankly, she's a bitch—calculating and conniving," she said as she ravaged the Pop-Tarts. "So did he ask you out?"

"Well, we've kind of been talking," Robin replied casually.

"He is one beautiful man, girl! Mmm… damn, girl, you need to get on that. He is fine!"

They both laughed and then settled back down to eat breakfast. A few quiet moments passed before Wendy continued. "From what I heard around the office, he really got shafted when Miss Thang divorced him. She cleaned him out. She was messin' around with some other guy. She ended up marrying him only a few days after the divorce was final. Sheryl and Matt have a daughter, though. I've never heard a bad word said about him around the hospital. It's always been bad stuff about her. Everybody says he is a good dad and a super-nice guy."

"Good."

"You were afraid he was a jerk, huh?"

Robin nodded. "Yeah."

"You know I don't pay attention to gossip, but because your feelings are involved, I'm going to tell you this too. You have to promise not to freak out, though."

Robin held her breath in anticipation.

"People around the office say they think Sheryl and Matt still have a thing going on. Matt doesn't date much. Everyone thinks that's strange because he's so handsome. From what I also hear, he's not gay. The women are practically throwing themselves at him. He doesn't pay attention, though."

This information wasn't what Robin wanted to hear. She couldn't hide her disappointed expression.

"Now don't do that," Wendy demanded. "It's just rumors. You give this man a fair chance. You deserve a little happiness."

"I just…" Robin trailed off.

"Stop it and finish the cereal, girl. It's just a rumor. It may not be true. Remember that before you go shuttin' doors. Don't let what people say get in your head. You use your own judgment. You're smart and intuitive."

"Thanks, Wendy. And I'm glad you told me everything."

4

As Tuesday evening's softball game approached, Robin was filled with anticipation. She and Wendy drove to the ball field together. They pulled onto the gravel lot, and when they arrived, disappointment rushed over Robin as she realized Matt's truck wasn't there. She wondered if he had decided not to come. She wondered if he had decided to stand her up. Insecurity turned to anger as she thought about how she didn't need the headache or worry of such trivial things.

A calm inner voice encouraged her to be positive. The conversation with Wendy had put her on edge. It had planted seeds of doubt in Robin's mind. She just knew she couldn't deal with more heartbreak. Drama was not her style either.

Little by little, the dugout filled with co-workers. Robin made her way over as Wendy stayed behind and spread out a blanket on the warm grass.

The police department's team congregated in the outfield. Colin Baker walked to the children's services dugout. He had an insatiable crush on Robin. He was kind with a great personality. She had always been aware of the crush, but she wasn't interested in him romantically.

He grinned. "Ankle doing okay?" he asked kindly.

She smiled as she watched his curly blond hair blow in the warm breeze. With a nod, she put weight on it. "I think I'll live. Thanks for asking. I can still run pretty fast, so you guys better watch out." She smirked.

"Well, I'll have to make sure I keep up with you this evening then." He laughed.

Soon, 6:00 turned to 6:15. Robin grew more irritated. The calming voice in her head was overridden by her frustration. Being stood up was humiliating, even if she was the only one who knew Matt had made plans to come.

As she stood in the outfield fuming, she heard the roar of a diesel engine and the gravel cracking under the tires. She glanced over to see the white truck pulling in. A sense of relief swept over her, but she was still put out by his tardiness.

The game started. After three strikes, the teams ran to their dugouts. Robin was parched. She made no effort to acknowledge Matt. She knew she was being childish and even a bit unreasonable. Still, her defenses and fear held her captive.

Robin noticed Matt walking toward the dugout. He wore a pair of dark-washed jeans with black Converse high-top tennis shoes. His plain gray T-shirt was snug against his frame as the wind blew against him. Nonchalantly, Robin turned her head in his direction. He smiled and waved. She smiled superficially and walked out of the dugout to meet him.

They met in the middle. "Hey," he said, "I'm sorry I was late. I went to the wrong field. When I realized kids were playing, I knew I was in the wrong place."

"It's okay," she lied.

"I'm sorry. I didn't want you to think I wasn't coming, so I tried to call your cell, but you must have already been on the field."

"Really, Matt, it's okay. Mistakes happen."

Robin realized she hadn't checked her cell phone before going onto the field. She suddenly felt ashamed.

"I was wondering if you might want to join me at the bowling alley tomorrow night. Some of the doctors and nurses formed a league. We meet in Oxford every Wednesday evening."

Pleased by the invitation, she beamed. "Sure. What time?"

"We start at 6:30 p.m. I usually go right to work afterward. Is it too much for you to just meet me there?"

"I don't mind meeting you there."

"Awesome," he concluded. "Well, I'll let you get back to it," he said as he waved and walked away.

Robin made her way back to the others in the dugout. She looked inside her bag and picked up her cell phone. Sure enough, there was a missed call from Matt at 6:03 p.m. A missed text came in at 6:08 p.m. She was relieved that she was wrong. She felt guilty for jumping to conclusions so quickly.

The game continued. Robin noticed that Matt and Wendy appeared to be in a deep conversation. She was curious. That made it hard for her to concentrate on her duties in the outfield.

During another break, Wendy came over to the dugout to talk to Terri, but Robin interrupted them.

"What were you talking about?" Robin asked bluntly.

"Huh?" Wendy asked.

"You and Matt. What were you talking about?"

Wendy hesitated. "Well, I just told him that you had been hurt, you know? And that he needed to be careful with you."

"Wendy!" Robin whispered harshly.

"What? I'm just trying to protect you."

"Oh my God! I can't leave you alone with anyone!"

"Oh, it's not that bad," Wendy retorted. "I just don't want to see you hurt anymore. Every man needs a good warning talk now and then."

Robin buried her face in her hands as she sat on the wooden bench. "Wendy," she said, "you have got to get a grip. Tell me what else you said!"

"I just told him if he wasn't in this for the right reasons, he should step off."

"Oh God," Robin sighed.

"I told him that you have been through a lot, but I didn't offer up any details. I told him that I knew you guys were just getting to know each other, but games weren't your style." She paused and then hesitantly continued. "And I also told him that if he was still hooking up with his ex-wife, to leave you out of it."

"Well, it sounds like you covered everything," she bit out.

Wendy threw up her hands. "Listen, if I scared him off with that, then he wasn't worth hanging onto anyway."

5

At the end of the game, the team met at a sports bar in town. Matt drove Robin to the restaurant. He complimented her on her performance in the game. He asked about her ankle. They talked about the concert plans. Matt's aftershave made it very difficult for Robin to stay on topic. She glanced over at him as he drove. It was hard to keep her eyes off him. He felt her staring and turned his head slightly to smile.

"What?" he asked.

She jumped a little, realizing she'd been caught looking at him. "Nothing," she answered with an innocent smile.

Before going into the bar, she took off her cleats and slipped on a pair of flip-flops. She knew she smelled like dust and sweat. This seemed to be a pattern for her. The first time she met Matt, she had been in the same condition. She looked forward to tomorrow night's bowling league. She could finally put on some nice clothing and perfume.

They walked into the restaurant and sat down with the team. Terri and Wendy sat beside Dalton Carver, Terri's best friend. Landon Phillips, an ongoing worker; Patricia Felix, the agency secretary; Carla Vincent, an ongoing worker in the delinquency unit; and Paul Riser, the intake supervisor, sat around the table. Laughter filled the room.

Matt pulled out a chair for Robin, and suddenly the laughter stopped, though the smiles continued.

"Everybody," Robin began, "this is Matt."

He was greeted warmly by members of the group.

The police department's team came and sat down with the children's services team. Colin sat across from Matt, making Robin feel awkward. But both Colin and Matt grinned cordially.

Pitchers of beer peppered the table, and orders were taken. Cheers could be heard throughout the bar as patrons watched the ball games on big screen TVs.

"You played like a champ tonight, Robin," Colin said sweetly. "Looks like that ankle really is fixed."

"She did play well, didn't she?" Matt said as he looked over at her with an adoring smile. Gently, he put his arm around the back of her chair.

"I was very impressed," he added.

She blushed at the compliment.

"So, what is it that you do?" Colin asked Matt candidly.

"I'm an E.R. doctor in Oxford."

"Cool," he said. "At least if Robin gets hurt, she's got someone to take care of her."

"Oh God, here we go," Robin said softly.

Confused, Matt glanced at the faces around the table. Everyone laughed, but Matt still didn't understand what he was missing.

"Robin has a real bad habit of tripping over her own feet," Paul explained. "I've seen her literally trip on the carpet when there was absolutely nothing there." The laughter grew louder. Robin felt Matt's eyes on her as she kept her head down bashfully.

"I will admit," she began as she finally looked up, "I'm not the most graceful creature, but I try, damn it." She turned her attention to him. "I told you I had two left feet."

The night continued comfortably, but 9:15 meant Matt needed to leave. He leaned over to Robin's ear. His breath against her earlobe sent goose bumps down her arms.

"I need to get going," he whispered.

She turned her face toward him. Their lips were merely inches away from each other.

"Okay," she answered. The lump in her throat almost made her mute. "I'll... I'll walk you out," she stuttered.

When he stood, everyone at the table sighed and booed.

"Leaving already?" one of them asked.

"Unfortunately, yes. I have to be at work in about forty-five minutes."

Everyone said good-bye. They told him how happy they were to meet him. Even Colin seemed to approve.

Matt walked out with Robin following. They stood outside the bar on the sidewalk. Robin dropped her head. "I'm glad you came," she said.

"Me, too. I'm really sorry I was late."

"Oh no, don't worry about it. I'm just glad you made it."

"It was fun. Your friends are hysterical, too."

"They're crazy, it's true," she said as her posture straightened, and she looked into his eyes.

"You're catching a ride with Wendy?"

"Yes. I am."

"Then I will see you tomorrow night, okay?"

"I will be there," she answered with a wave and a smile. She turned and returned to her friends inside the bar.

6

Robin walked into the cool air-conditioned agency. She didn't remember May ever being so humid. She flopped into her office chair and gazed up at the clock. It was 3:50 p.m., and 4:30 didn't seem to be coming fast enough.

Paul walked into her tiny office and sat down in the vacant chair. He saw her fatigued scowl.

Paul was a tall, thin man. His career started years ago in mental health. He gravitated toward children's services work in the late '70s and found his niche. He had always been fair to work for. The investigations staff respected him a great deal.

"Hey Robin, you have a minute?" he asked.

"Sure," she answered. "What's up?"

Paul paused and inhaled.

"Well," he began, "I'm retiring. I want you to be the first to know."

"Retiring? When?"

"I gave my notice today. In a month, I'll be gone."

"Is everything okay?"

"It's just time. I've been in this business for a long time, Robin. My wife and I want to travel. Halie is getting married and my other daughter is pregnant with our first grandchild."

"Wow." Robin was surprised. "Well, we'll miss you. You've been a great mentor, Paul. I couldn't have asked for a better teacher."

"I'm going to be very frank with you, Robin." He continued, "I want you to apply for the supervisor's position when it's posted."

"Me?"

"You are more than capable of doing the job."

"What about the others? They have seniority."

"Seniority doesn't matter. We aren't a union agency. Capability, leadership, and respect matter more than who's been here the longest anyway. The money is better, and you won't have to be bothered with the pager all the time. Of course, you'll carry the supervisor's pager, but it doesn't come with the same pressures. It's a lot to consider, I know, and a lot more responsibility. But I know you. I know your work. You were made for the job."

"I don't know," she said, shaking her head.

"Please."

"I thought Jim Kelsing was next in line."

"Listen to me. If I have anything to do with it, I'll pull for you. You are so good at this, Robin. You truly love the work. You're great with your families. I wish everyone showed your kind of devotion. Jim's burned out." He paused. "You just give it some thought, okay? The position won't be posted for another week. So, you have some time to mull it over."

After work, Robin went home to change and then headed to the bowling alley. She enjoyed watching Matt and his friends. She welcomed the distraction. Her heart felt heavy as she contemplated Paul's proposal. She'd never considered becoming a supervisor. She felt inadequate for such heavy responsibilities.

When the evening ended, Matt walked Robin to her car. He nonchalantly took her hand. She turned to him and smiled. Still, she was obviously preoccupied. Matt quickly picked it up, too.

"What's going on in that head of yours?" he asked.

"What?"

"You're distracted."

She shrugged. "Do you remember Paul?"

"Sure. The older bald guy."

"He told me that he is retiring. He wants me to apply for the supervisor's position."

"That's good, isn't it?"

"It certainly has its benefits. It's much better pay. I wouldn't have to be on call as often either."

"That would be a plus, right?"

"Yes. I just don't know if I can handle all of the responsibilities. I don't feel like I know the laws and the regulations well enough. I just don't know if I'm capable."

They arrived at her car. She broke away from Matt and leaned against her old Ford Bronco. She felt defeated, as if the decision had already been made.

Matt smiled. "Change is something that isn't always welcomed. Human beings hate it. We fight against it. Change is the only way we can evolve. It's the way we grow."

Robin smirked. "You sound like a philosopher."

Matt stood beside Robin and leaned against the car. "Robin, you've got grit. I haven't known you that long, but I know you're brilliant. You work so hard. I think you have a lot of qualities that would make you a great leader." He nudged her. "I'm biased, though."

She grinned as she looked over at him. "Thanks for the pep talk, Matt," she said.

"Anytime." He looked into her beautiful eyes. They held so much mystery.

"I need to get going," Robin said as she unlocked the car door. "Talk to you tomorrow?" she asked.

"Absolutely." He hesitated but moved in closer. "You know," he continued, "I don't feel like we've really been out on a date just yet, so the only kiss I will offer is one that's very old-fashioned. My dad always said that a lady loved to be kissed on the hand. My dad was a hopeless romantic, so I'm betting he was right," he said as he gently took Robin's hand and brought it to his lips. Never losing eye contact, he kissed her knuckles.

Robin's pulse sped. Her cheeks flushed pink. "That's very chivalrous of you," she commented. "I think your dad gave really great advice," she concluded.

He softly released her hand. "I'm glad you were able to make it tonight," he said. "I planned to come to your softball game tomorrow night, but my daughter has a soccer game."

"Oh, that's fine."

"I will call you, okay? Let me know when you make it home safe."

She nodded as she opened the car door. She slipped inside and closed it. With a polite wave, she drove out of the parking lot, exhilarated by her evening with Matt.

7

Matt sat down on his couch after a long night working in the E.R. He yearned for his bed. Still, his mind needed to settle down before he could even consider sleeping.

He grabbed his phone and keyed in a text to Robin: *Good morning, beautiful. Sleep well?* As he checked his emails on his phone, a response came through: *I slept well. How was work?*

He typed a response: *Long. I'm glad to be home. I will get online around 7:30 tonight if you wanna chat. I should be back from Olivia's game by that time.*

Robin responded: *Sounds like a plan. Sleep well.*

He replied: *Will do. Be safe out there today.*

A knock at his front door startled him. He looked up. His best friend, Bill Kindell, stood at the threshold, waving. Matt motioned for him to come in. Bill pulled open the screen door and smiled.

Bill was an EMT for one of the local ambulance companies. Matt and Bill had become quick friends because they were always running into one another in the E.R.

Bill was Latino. He was much shorter than Matt, with curly jet-black hair and tanned skin. He was very well-liked and respected among his peers. He had a lot of friends and connections with a lot of folks in influential positions in the community. So, Matt sought his help in finding out more about Robin. He wanted to make sure she was truthful. Even though he felt a little guilty asking Bill to dig, Matt knew Bill would be able to find out anything about Robin that Matt should be aware of.

Matt stood and walked to the kitchen. "You want some coffee?" he asked.

Bill sat down in the recliner. "No, man. I'm good. That was one hell of a shift, though. I lost count of how many times I saw you last night. I hate when it's a full moon."

Matt walked back in with the cup in his hand. He sat down on the couch and then took a sip.

"Well, I did some digging on your girlfriend," Bill started.

"Not my girlfriend, Bill."

"Dude, lighten up," he scolded. "Anyway, Robin May Hillard has no criminal history. She is who she says she is. Her education checks out. No previous marriages. No children. Comes from a small town in Southern Ohio, just like she said. I know why her friend gave you such a heavy-handed warning, though."

Anticipation rose as Matt put his coffee cup on the end table.

"Robin had a boyfriend who was not such a great guy. They lived in Hamilton for a time. He sent her to the hospital a couple of times with some broken ribs. She claimed she'd fallen. A few years ago, the dude held her hostage in their apartment. He almost killed her. He's in jail now. Your Robin," Bill continued, "she's really been through it, but damn, she's strong. Still, I'd handle with care if you know what I mean."

Matt shook his head in disgust. He was angry that someone could do that to her. "How could someone…" he trailed off.

Bill leaned up with his elbows on his knees. "It's obvious that you really like this girl."

Matt nodded.

"She checks out, Matt. She seems like a real good lady."

"Good," Matt said with a nod. "Just knowing how badly she's been hurt makes me want to protect her."

"I figured that is how you'd react," Bill said.

"It cuts me knowing she was almost killed. Now I understand why she seems to tread so lightly. She seems to want to keep me at arm's length."

"That'd be why. Who could blame her?" Bill said with a shrug.

"My advice to you would be to make sure she's what you're looking for. She's got a lot of baggage, and we both know that comes with some challenges."

Matt nodded again. "Yeah. She seems to have everything handled, though."

"That might be true, but you all are just getting to know each other. Just be careful, man. I just don't want to see you hurt," Bill added.

The visit with Bill shed some light on the situation. Still, it didn't change the trajectory for Matt. He was still interested in getting to know Robin.

Each day that passed allowed Matt and Robin to talk on the phone, text, and chat online. Conversations enlightened both of them to quirks and interests. They communicated well and enjoyed the hours of conversation.

8

The day of the concert finally arrived. Robin stood in front of the mirror, taking account of her appearance. Her reflection failed to put her at ease. With Wendy's help, Robin picked out a colorful top with a halter tie and a pair of black capri pants. She borrowed Wendy's black cross-band wedge sandals. Because of the heat, Robin twisted her hair up. The small silver hoops hung from her ears, bringing the entire outfit together nicely.

She heard his truck pull into the parking lot. Adrenaline rushed through her veins as she anticipated seeing him. She walked to the window and peeked out. Matt was shutting his truck off. She watched him step out and walk toward the apartment.

She closed the curtain and sat down on her bed. She heard the knock at the front door and Wendy's voice. Then Terri's. Robin felt paralyzed by anxiety. She trembled slightly. Finally, Wendy opened the bedroom door.

"He's here," Wendy whispered.

"Do you think this is too much?" Robin asked, gesturing at her outfit. "I don't want to look slutty."

"No way. You look like lava, baby," Wendy answered softly. "Go have fun. He is looking sexy." She winked. "He's so hot he could light a firecracker."

"So remind me again why he's even remotely interested in me?"

"Stop that," Wendy scolded as she sat beside her. "You are a beautiful, successful woman. Quit thinking you're not good enough. Aren't you the one who always says your past doesn't define you?"

Robin nodded. "I know you're right. I'm sorry."

"You don't have to be sorry, doll. Just take all this in and have a good time. Let him spoil you. If he doesn't do it for you, move on. If he disrespects you, get out. You know?"

Robin nodded, gathering the courage to stand and walk to the bedroom door. She opened it and made her way down the hallway to the living room.

Matt stood in the middle of the room wearing light-washed boot-cut jeans, a short-sleeved graphic T-shirt, and navy-blue Converse high tops. His mouth opened slightly at the sight of Robin.

"Wow," he whispered.

Robin felt her face warm as she blushed. She smiled sweetly. "Ready?" she asked.

He stood silently, still staring.

"What?" she asked.

He blinked. "What happened?"

She giggled, flattered by his reaction.

"Oh yeah. We have a concert to get to, right?" he joked, pulling himself together. He walked to the front door, held open the screen, and let her step out first. As they crossed the parking lot, he quickly stepped ahead to open the passenger door for her.

"You look sensational," he said.

"Thank you. You look great," she replied.

He smiled as she hopped into the cab.

They talked the entire way to the venue. When they arrived at the amphitheater, Matt found a spot, parked, and hopped out. He rounded the truck and opened her door again. Robin stepped out and leaned lightly against the bed of the truck. Matt approached her and smiled.

"I just want you to know," he said softly as he took her hand, "I'm so glad you came with me tonight."

The butterflies in her stomach took flight. "I was looking forward to it," she said.

He leaned closer. "I've been waiting two weeks to be with you like this. Before we go any further..." He smirked. "Can I kiss you?"

Robin nodded, unable to find her voice.

He caressed her cheek, brushed a strand of hair away, and smiled. "You're so beautiful," he whispered. He cupped her face and leaned in. Their lips met for the first time, tender, exhilarating.

When they pulled away, he took her hand. "As much as I'd love to stay out here and keep going with this," he said, "we have a concert to attend. Bill and Leah are probably wondering where the hell we are."

Robin nodded as she bit her bottom lip.

Matt led them through the crowd toward the entrance. Bill waved as he stood with his girlfriend, Leah Wilson. Matt introduced Robin, and as they waited in line, they all made small talk.

Leah was a tall, beautiful blonde with big blue eyes and fair skin. She wore ripped jeans and a concert T-shirt, flip-flops, and her hair in a braid. She seemed like a free spirit, and Robin liked that about her.

They found a spot on the grass. Bill and Matt spread out blankets while Robin and Leah sat with their legs crossed.

"Do you ladies want something to drink?" Bill asked.

"Whiskey sour," Leah answered.

"If they have Mike's Hard Lemonade, I'll take one," Robin said, glancing at Matt.

"Got it," he said. Bill and Matt walked off toward the concession stand.

Robin watched them until they were out of sight. She took in the surroundings—the sunset painting the sky with purple, orange, and red.

Leah lay back on the blanket. "You two make a cute couple," she began.

"Thanks."

"Bill is always talking about how Matt needs to get involved with someone nice."

"Everyone needs someone nice," Robin agreed.

"You seem like a good person. God knows it's about time Matt found someone who wasn't a barracuda. His ex-wife is a nightmare."

Robin felt a pit form in her stomach. "She is?"

"God, yes. When we doubled, she was always disrespectful and condescending. But have you met their little girl? She doesn't look a thing like Matt. I'm guessing she's not even his."

Robin was stunned by Leah's bluntness.

Meanwhile, in line, Matt's phone buzzed. He glanced at the screen. Sheryl. He shook his head.

"You need to squash that, man," Bill warned. "She's gonna swoop in and ruin this. She always does."

"Not this time."

"What's different?"

"It just feels different with Robin."

"Then squash it. Don't let Sheryl blow this up."

Back on the hill, Matt and Bill zigzagged through the crowd carrying drinks. Matt handed Robin her lemonade and sat beside her. Their eyes locked. He leaned in and kissed her softly.

Robin beamed. "That was unexpected. Are you the affectionate type?"

"Guilty," he said. "Is that okay?"

Robin nodded. "It's very okay."

The concert lasted three hours. Afterward, they all decided to go to a nightclub in Oxford. The place was filled with college students, many of whom seemed to know Matt.

They found a booth. Robin admitted she wasn't hungry. She was uncomfortable—between the crowd, the attention Matt received, and the looming dance floor.

Matt leaned into her ear. "If you want to go…"

"Oh no, it's fine. I'm just a terrible dancer."

"I won't let you fall," he said with a wink.

A waitress arrived wearing a tight, sequined top and a miniskirt. She openly ogled Matt the entire time. Robin ordered an Old

Fashioned, knowing she'd need courage for dancing and for dealing with the swarm of women who seemed drawn to Matt.

When the drinks arrived, the waitress winked at Matt. Robin rolled her eyes. Matt caught it immediately.

"I have to warn you," Robin said, staring into her drink. "I'm a cheap drunk."

"You're in good hands," Matt reassured her.

Soon after, Bill and Leah escaped to the dance floor. A tall redhead slid into the empty seat beside Matt.

"Doc Gregory!" she squealed. "Haven't seen you in forever!"

Matt greeted her politely, but Robin felt her stomach tighten. She'd been with someone like this before. Someone every woman flocked to. It had not ended well.

Finally, Matt took Robin's hand and set it on the table. "This is Robin. Robin, this is Gail."

Gail gave a tight, insincere smile. "Pleasure," she said sharply.

When a slow song began, Matt used it as an exit strategy. "If you'll excuse us, I think I'm going to take this lovely lady to the dance floor."

On the floor, he wrapped his arms around her and held her close. He kissed her forehead and traced the exposed skin on her back.

"You can trust me, you know," he said.

She remained silent.

"You're afraid to trust me."

"If I had a penny for every time I've heard that one…"

"I know. You'd be rich."

"Matt… I've been through some things. I don't want to go through them again."

"Are you comfortable sharing?"

She sighed. "I was with someone who seemed perfect. But as time went on, he became violent. I missed all the signs. He hurt me, physically and emotionally. There are days I feel like I'm never going to be quite right. Like I'm damaged. I've been in therapy a long time, and things are more manageable now… but the injuries are still there. And not everyone can handle that."

Matt smiled softly. "Thank you for telling me. I appreciate that you felt like you could."

"I also feel like your ex-wife might be an issue," she admitted gently.

"Absolutely not. Things have been over for a long time. She isn't my problem. My daughter is my priority."

"I just worried you still carried a torch for her. I can't compete with a ghost."

"You don't have to. I promise."

He stopped dancing, cupped her face, and kissed her gently.

They left the club at 2:30 a.m. Matt drove Robin home. In the truck, they sat quietly. Despite his reassurances, Robin still worried about his intentions.

"Do you mind if I walk you to your door?" he asked.

"Not at all."

He helped her out of the truck and walked her up the stairs.

"Tonight was great," he said.

"It was," Robin agreed.

"If you want, I'll come to your next softball game, but only under one condition."

"A condition?" she asked with a smile.

"You have to come to my bowling league on Wednesdays."

"If that's what you'd like, then sure."

Matt stepped closer and kissed her—deeper, more intimate, more certain than before. Then he kissed her forehead.

"I'll text you when I'm home," he whispered.

She nodded as he walked down the stairs. The engine roared to life, and he drove away, leaving Robin alone with her memories and her thoughts.

9

It was Monday morning. Robin sat in her office staring at her computer screen, lost in thought as she reminisced about the weekend. She closed her eyes as she recalled the touch of Matt's lips on hers. A knock at her door startled her back to reality.

"Come in," she said pleasantly as she opened her eyes.

Colin Baker popped his head in. "Hey there," he said as he walked in and sat in the vacant chair beside her desk. He wore his uniform, so she assumed he needed to talk to her about a case.

"Hey. What's up?" Robin asked courteously.

"Why does anything have to be up? Can't a friend drop in and say hello?"

"Of course," Robin said as she pushed away from her desk. "Seriously though, you never come by. What's going on?"

"It's about your new boyfriend," he blurted out.

"Okay," Robin said apprehensively.

"Oh, it's nothing bad," Colin clarified. "I just know what you've been through. I was there, remember?"

"How could I forget?" Robin asked in a somber tone.

"I just want him to be good to you. You've been through enough. I will always have your back, Robin. I hope you know that."

She nodded. "I know."

Her mind wandered back to that fateful day in Hamilton. It played in her mind like a movie reel—a horror film on repeat. She remembered him losing control. She remembered the sound of the gun cabinet opening. She recalled the feeling of the barrel against her forehead. In her mind, she heard his voice shouting, "You won't leave me!" Then she remembered the apartment door crashing open, police wrestling him to the ground. They cuffed him and took him away, leaving Robin trembling in the living room corner. Colin had been the one to offer comfort and refuge.

"You haven't dated a lot," Colin reminded her. "You've put up some pretty high walls. I just want to make sure that whoever you take them down for is worthy of it. You deserve nothing but the best."

"I appreciate that, Colin. It means a lot. I don't think you have to worry about Matt though."

"I checked him out," he admitted.

"You ran a background check on him? That's not even legal," Robin said, shocked.

"I didn't run an official check. Don't get all worked up," Colin assured her. "Either way, Matt's record is clean."

"Well, that's good." Robin's expression softened. "I appreciate that you're looking out for me. You're a good friend."

"Friend…" Colin said with a disappointed sigh. "I guess I'd hoped we could be more eventually. I'm too late though. You always intimidated me."

Robin's mouth dropped open. "Intimidated you? Are you serious?"

"Well, yeah," he shrugged. "You're so smart and put together. I just thought you'd never be interested in a guy like me."

Robin rolled her chair toward him and placed her hand on his. "Colin, I'm so sorry. I didn't know."

"It's okay. You couldn't have known. I didn't tell ya. Kept it to myself." He dropped his head. "I just want you to be happy, even if it isn't me that has a hand in that."

"I wish you would have said something," Robin admitted.

"Would it have changed anything?" Colin asked.

Robin thought quietly for a moment and then pursed her lips.

"Exactly," he said.

Robin felt horrible for rejecting Colin. However, the visit served as an important reminder. Colin had let his opportunities pass him by. In spite of her fear, Robin wanted to make a genuine effort with Matt. She couldn't let the chance pass her by. She had to give him the opportunity to show her who he really was.

In the spirit of moving toward a more serious path with Matt, Robin talked to him every day in some way. Between texting, calling, and chatting, they were building a foundation.

Every Tuesday night, Matt attended Robin's softball games, and every Wednesday night Robin met him at the bowling alley. On the weekends that Matt's daughter didn't visit, Robin spent time with him. Each moment revealed more things they had in common. Respect grew between them. Still, Robin avoided intimacy. Luckily, Matt was patient. Kissing here and there, holding hands, snuggling up for a movie. Those were her comfort limits, and he honored them.

Robin interviewed for the supervisor's position at the end of June. The department felt different without Paul. Jennifer Sutton had been filling in. With schools out for the summer, caseloads thinned, making Jennifer's job easier.

Soon it was July. Matt asked Robin to go with him to Middletown for Independence Day. She gladly agreed. She met his mother, Doris, and his brother Charlie, along with Tammy, Charlie's wife.

Doris was a hearty woman who commanded respect in the way she carried herself. Only 5'3", she had shiny grey hair and deep brown eyes. She was strong and capable, and it didn't surprise Robin that she still lived alone.

Robin and Doris sat on the porch watching cars go by. Matt, Charlie, and Tammy went into town to run errands and pick up food for the family reunion. Robin sensed Doris watching her and turned her head.

"You know," Doris began, "there's something special about you."

"Oh?" Robin asked.

"Yes. Matthew has been through a lot. I watched him tear himself apart during his divorce, especially when Sheryl tried to sue for full custody. He tormented himself. He blamed himself. You seem to have brought healing to him. He just adores you, Robin. I haven't seen him smile like this since he was young."

"I can't tell you how happy I am to hear that," Robin said. "He means a lot to me. I know we've only been dating a short time, but I feel like he's always been a part of my life."

Doris grinned. "That's how it should be. Their presence in your life should feel familiar." She closed her eyes briefly and then continued. "Meeting Matt's father was my destiny. He'd just been discharged from the service. Handsome fellow. I met him at a charity auction. That man could light up a room with a smile. I felt like he was divine, like he was sent straight from heaven just for me."

"That's so romantic."

"You have that same way about you. I can see it," Doris explained. "Matthew can see it too. He sees the soul. I think medicine and science have clouded his ability to think about the bigger picture, though. We're certainly not alone in this life's journey, are we?"

Robin nodded. "I know I'm not alone. I think we all get lost from time to time. Then when we finally find our truest self and our dearest love, we appreciate it more. It makes the journey's end that much sweeter."

"I think you're exactly right. What a brilliant way to put it," Doris said.

After meeting Matt's extended family and enjoying the Fourth of July festivities, Robin returned to work. The week dragged on. Two sexual abuse cases came in, keeping her busy with case notes and summaries for the police department.

Robin's primary job in intake had always been sexual abuse investigations. She'd been specially trained in interviewing techniques. She gained rapport easily with children and had become an expert in preparing them for court.

Robin's desk phone buzzed. She answered and heard Shawn Portman's voice summoning her to his office. The request made her nervous.

Shawn had been the director for fifteen years, navigating political struggles and maintaining the agency's reputation. He always seemed to come out on top.

Robin pushed the door open slowly. Seated at the large table were Shawn, assistant director Monica Valence, and Paul. A vacant chair sat at the end of the table.

"Have a seat, Robin," Shawn said.

She sat down and folded her hands in her lap. The lump in her throat made it hard to swallow.

Shawn began. "Robin, we carefully considered all the candidates for Paul's job." A long pause followed. "We'd like to offer the position to you."

"Really?" She lit up.

"Yes," Monica said. "You are very qualified. We reviewed your education and recommendations. You are unquestionably the best candidate."

"Do you need time to think about it?" Paul asked.

"Not at all!"

"As we explained in the interview, the salary is $65,000 a year," Shawn added.

Robin nodded.

"Sixty thousand is the base rate," Monica clarified. "Five thousand is for the on-call responsibilities. In a year, you'll be reviewed for a raise."

"The on-call duties are split among supervisors," Shawn added. "Your benefits won't change. You'll attend supervisor trainings. Each month we have an administrative brunch. There will be other responsibilities, but we don't want to overwhelm you."

"I understand," she said gratefully.

"Congratulations, Robin," Paul said proudly.

After discussing a few more details, Robin returned to her office and grabbed her phone. She quickly texted Matt:

I got it! I'm the new supervisor!

Her phone buzzed immediately.

"I am so proud of you! Congratulations!" Matt exclaimed when she answered.

"Thank you so much!"

"You're beautiful and successful and smart. I am truly the luckiest man alive."

"You're making me blush."

"We're celebrating! I'm taking you out for a really nice dinner tonight. Dress up. It's a nice place. I'll be over at six-thirty."

"Matt, you don't have to—"

"I insist. This is a big deal. We need to celebrate."

"Alright, alright. I won't fuss. I'll see you this evening."

.

10

Robin stood in her bedroom looking over her wardrobe. "I have nothing!" she shouted.

Wendy came in with a few dresses. "I've got you covered, girl. Don't you worry." She laid the dresses on the bed and spread them out so Robin could make an informed choice. Undoubtedly, it was the black cocktail dress, elegant yet simple.

"I like that one," Robin said, pointing at it.

"Let me go get some accessories," Wendy said excitedly.

As Robin stood in the middle of the room, the reality of her situation sank in. She was exhilarated. The supervisor's position meant a number of things to her. She could finally purchase a new car, which she desperately needed. She could pay off her student loans more quickly. Other bills and debts could be wiped out. She could focus more on saving money for her future.

Wendy walked back in with a pearl necklace and matching earrings. "You can also borrow my black sandals with the heels. They look great with this dress."

"Hair up or down?" Robin asked.

Wendy contemplated with a finger to her chin. "Mmm. If you're going to an elegant place, you'll wanna wear it up."

"I don't know where we're going. He does this a lot. He tells me to be ready at a certain time for a date, and then he surprises me with where he takes me," Robin explained.

Wendy folded her arms. "I think that's the most romantic thing I've ever heard."

"Should I wear lingerie? We haven't even made out. I don't know if we'll have sex tonight or not. He's been so patient."

Wendy walked to the bed and moved the other dresses out of the way. "Are you kidding me? You haven't slept together yet?"

Robin shook her head.

"My mama always told me to be prepared for anything, so I say wear some sexy-ass underwear at least," Wendy suggested. "Is the chemistry just not there?"

Robin nodded. "Oh yes. The chemistry is there. I think he is the sexiest man alive. My God, the way he smiles at me…"

"So why have you all held off?" Wendy asked curiously.

Robin walked to her desk, pulled out the chair, and sat down. "I'm afraid. Sex changes everything. It always does. It complicates things. I like the lightness of our relationship right now. Once we have sex, everything will get heavy."

"You've obviously never had sex with the right man," Wendy refuted. "Sex is supposed to strengthen the relationship. Robin, you're basically a therapist. You know this."

Robin nodded guiltily. "I know. I just don't want things to get difficult for us."

"If he's the right guy, it won't become difficult." Wendy got up, grabbing the cocktail dress from the bed. "Get dressed," she said as she handed the outfit to Robin. "Put on some sexy shit underneath. Dab that perfume you love on your collarbone, on your nipples, and on your inner thighs. Girl, you need to be set. It's almost six, so you'd best get hoppin'."

Robin quickly prepared for her date. She even took Wendy's advice. Wendy left a matching clutch on the dresser. Robin grabbed it and walked down the hallway to the living room. She heard the knock at the door and nervously opened it.

Matt stood on the other side of the screen door in a black tuxedo. His hair was smoothed back. He held a bundle of flowers in his hand.

Robin opened the screen as Matt stepped inside. She caught a faint whiff of his cologne. It was intoxicating. Her mind drifted for a moment to what their first sexual experience might be like, but she quickly came back to reality.

"My, my, Dr. Gregory," she began calmly. "You look rather debonair tonight."

He nodded slowly as he took in her appearance. "You look ravishing," he said softly.

"I'm surprised to see a tux. This must be a fancy place you're whisking me off to."

"Are you impressed?" he asked with a smirk.

"Very," she nodded.

"Are you turned on?"

"You could say that." She blushed.

"We have to do this more often then," he said with a devious grin.

Wendy came into the room and saw the two of them. With a wide smile, she said, "I'll take the flowers for you. You all get going."

They both nodded and walked out the door.

On the way there, it was quiet between them. Robin enjoyed holding Matt's hand as he rested it on his lap. She watched the passing cars outside the window. They stayed on the interstate for a long while before finally taking an exit outside Cincinnati.

Matt pulled into a parking lot where valets waited. He stepped out as one of them opened Robin's door and helped her onto the sidewalk.

She looked up at the sign above the restaurant. It was The Ledge House. She knew it was popular among influential people, difficult to reserve, and extremely expensive. Even so, she was flattered.

"Matt, this is too much," she said.

"We're celebrating. Enjoy it," he told her as their eyes met. "When will I be able to convince you that you're worth it?"

They walked toward the entrance and were greeted by a tall man behind a podium.

"Dr. Gregory. Good to see you," the man said.

"Hello, Jack. I have a reservation for two," Matt replied.

"Right this way, sir." Jack turned to grab the menus and led them through the restaurant and up a winding staircase. At the top was a large room with an entire wall of windows. Chandeliers hung from the ceiling. An elegant dance floor sat in the middle of the space. Candlelit tables were spread throughout the room. Quiet conversations drifted through the air.

Robin's mouth fell open. "Jesus Christ," she whispered. She felt Matt's hand on the small of her back as he guided her to the table.

The host pulled out her seat. After she sat, he took the artistically folded napkin from the table and placed it gently in her lap. He recited the wine specials and excused himself.

Robin looked down at the table. She'd never seen so many pieces of silverware before. Her expression must have given her away because Matt leaned in to whisper, "Go from the outside in."

She nodded while taking in the atmosphere. Many couples were waltzing on the dance floor. The dim lighting enhanced the romantic mood. Robin had never been anywhere quite like this.

A waitress arrived promptly. Matt ordered champagne.

"What are we celebrating?" the waitress asked.

"A well-deserved promotion," he answered as he smirked at Robin.

The waitress nodded and left the table.

Matt reached across and took Robin's hands. "I'm so proud of you," he said quietly. "You truly deserve this. You've worked hard."

Her cheeks warmed. "Thanks."

"You're so beautiful when you blush. You do it all the time."

"I'm blushing?" she asked, then apologized quickly. "I'm sorry."

"Don't be. It suits you." He lifted one of her hands and kissed her knuckles. "You deserve compliments. I know you have trouble believing that."

She nodded, but the waitress returned with their champagne before she could respond. They ordered dinner. When the plates arrived, they ate quietly, enjoying both the food and the ambiance.

Robin kept admiring the couples dancing and the violin quartet in the corner. The melodies filled the room with softness and charm.

Matt noticed her focus. "Dance with me," he said as he set his napkin down.

Shock washed over her face. She frowned and shook her head. "Matt, you know I can't."

"We danced before and you did fine. Leading is my job. You just follow."

"Really, Matt. This is a bad idea."

"Let's live dangerously," he said with raised eyebrows.

"Me dancing is dangerous."

Matt stood and offered his hand. She took it and rose to her feet. He led her to the dance floor and pulled her close. He was dazzled by her. She was mesmerized by him. The pull between them felt new and powerful.

After they finished their evening at the restaurant, they drove back to her apartment complex. Robin's thoughts ran wild. She thought about what Wendy had told her. Then she looked over at Matt. The dashboard lights cast a faint glow across his features. She studied his silhouette and the strong angle of his jaw.

He always took charge. His confidence made her feel safe. She admired that. She wondered how he'd been so patient with her. Sex hadn't always been a positive experience for her. She still struggled with how to navigate intimacy. Even so, she wanted to try with him. She simply didn't know how to express that.

Matt parked the truck and turned off the engine. He shifted in his seat to face her.

"As usual, I had a great time," she said politely. "Thank you for dinner. You really didn't have to do all that."

"It was a gift to you." He paused to take her in. "Can I say something without scaring you?"

"Scaring me?"

He took her hands. They trembled slightly. She was surprised by how nervous he seemed.

"These past two months have been the best of my life," he confessed.

"Mine too," she agreed. "It's been fun."

He lowered his gaze. His expression shifted. "Is that all it's been? Fun?"

"What do you mean?"

"I think you're afraid that I'm playing games with you. The truth is, I'm afraid you might be playing games with me."

"Oh no, Matt. I'm not. I'd never do that."

"How do I know?"

She shrugged. "I guess you don't. You can only judge by my behavior. If I felt like you were playing with me, I wouldn't be here. I think you know that."

"That's fair," he said quietly. "But I'm curious. Where do you see this going? What do you think the future looks like for us?"

She felt cornered. They were still getting to know each other. "I don't know."

Matt exhaled heavily. He lifted his eyes again. "I know you don't want to be hurt. I know you're afraid I'm not who I appear to be. You think I might hurt you or turn cruel. But I could never be cruel to you. You matter too much." He turned her hand over and traced the lines in her palm.

"What about the shifts we work?" Robin asked. "Do you know how hard it'll be to maintain a relationship?"

"I think we've done well so far. Don't you?"

She nodded faintly.

"There are no guarantees in life," he continued. "I don't know what'll happen in a week or a month or a year. I know you still worry about my ex-wife. I know you doubt yourself and wrestle with your own trauma. And I know you're nervous about intimacy."

She was stunned by how accurately he read her.

"I'm not trying to rush sex," Matt said. "I think you know that. I'm very attracted to you, but I've let you take the lead. I didn't want to pressure you. I can wait. But I want you. I want you more than I've wanted anyone."

Robin touched his cheek. "I want you too," she whispered.

"I knew we could make this work if we had a little faith. If our schedules get too chaotic, I'll switch to days. I want to see where this takes us."

"So do I."

He placed his palm on her cheek and kissed her forehead, then her cheek, and finally her lips. The heat between them rose quickly. Robin pulled away long enough to find her voice.

"I believe you, Matt. You're good." She swallowed. "I'm sorry you've been paying for someone else's mistakes."

"I don't mind paying if I get you in the end."

They stared at each other quietly. Their fingers intertwined. He kissed her again. The kiss deepened. Robin felt her restraint melting. Her fear faded into desire.

She pulled away slightly, breathing unsteadily. She wanted this. She wanted him.

"Come inside," she whispered.

"You're sure?"

She nodded. "Yes. I'm sure."

They got out of the truck and walked up the stairs. Matt stood behind Robin as she fished in her purse for her keys. His warmth pressed against her back and made the anticipation rise within her. She felt his lips touch the back of her neck as his fingers grazed her shoulders, sending shivers through her body.

She finally unlocked the door. She tossed her purse and keys onto the end table and took Matt's hand. She led him down the short hallway toward her bedroom. They were alone. Wendy was staying with Terri, and Robin knew the entire night belonged to them.

She opened her bedroom door and let Matt step inside first. She shut the door behind them. The nightlight on her dresser cast a soft glow across the room, just enough to see without ruining the intimacy.

They met in the middle of the room and stood facing each other. With a gentle touch, Matt traced his fingers along Robin's forearms and then down to her wrists. She closed her eyes, feeling everything at once. He moved closer and kissed her. It started delicate and then deepened into something fierce. She wrapped her arms around his neck while his hands found the curves of her waist.

Robin stepped back and slipped off her sandals. Matt leaned down to untie his shoes, taking them off and setting them aside. Robin walked to the edge of the bed and sat. She watched as he removed his tuxedo jacket and placed it over the back of her desk chair. He loosened the bowtie and set it aside. Then he began unbuttoning his shirt. Robin stood as he opened it completely, revealing his chest and abdomen.

She ran her hands over his torso. Her heart pounded. He kissed her again. He then turned her gently and slid the zipper of her dress down until the fabric pooled at her feet. She turned back toward him, shy and unable to meet his eyes. She stood in a black lace strapless bra and matching thong.

Matt lifted her chin with one finger. "You're beautiful, Robin."

He took her hand and led her to the bed. She sat on the mattress while he knelt between her legs. He caressed her thighs and leaned up to kiss her again, his touch warm and deliberate. She curled her fingers through his hair, feeling the moment deepen. His fingertips moved to the hooks of her bra and loosened them. The fabric slipped away, exposing her. He cupped her breasts gently as their desire intensified.

Robin shifted backward onto the mattress and lay down. She watched as Matt removed his pants and underwear, his body strong and steady. He leaned over her. She reached out and touched him, her breath catching.

"I want you inside me," she whispered.

Matt removed her thong slowly and tossed it aside.

"Get into my top dresser drawer," Robin instructed softly. "There are condoms in there."

He nodded and did as she asked. He tore open a package and rolled one on, then moved between her legs. He took his time, touching her gently and preparing her.

Robin felt excitement flutter through her stomach. Their eyes stayed locked as he leaned in and slowly entered her. The connection stole her breath.

He balanced on his forearms and kissed her deeply. She wrapped her legs around him as he moved with her. His breath warmed her neck as he whispered, "You feel incredible."

"So do you," she said, her voice unsteady as pleasure built.

"You're close," he murmured.

She nodded with parted lips. She gripped his biceps as his rhythm shifted. He held himself above her and watched her body respond to each movement. Her skin flushed. Her back arched.

"Come with me," he said with urgency.

Robin moaned as the climax overtook her. Matt followed a heartbeat later, groaning as he pressed into her fully. Afterward, he rolled to the side and rested, breathless and warm. Robin gazed at him as she calmed, her body tingling. Sweat glimmered on his skin.

He felt her watching and turned his head to her. He opened his eyes and smiled. "You're amazing," he whispered.

She smiled back. "So are you."

"Can I use your bathroom?" he asked.

"Of course. Down the hall. First door on your right."

Robin went to Wendy's bathroom to clean up as well. When she returned to her room, she removed the comforter and slid under the sheets. She wanted Matt to stay, but she didn't want to seem clingy. Even so, she waited quietly for him to come back.

Matt entered and shut the door behind him. He walked to the bed and crawled in beside her. "Come here," he said softly.

She moved into his arms without hesitation. She rested her head on his chest while he traced his fingertips gently along her spine.

"You feel like home," he whispered.

She lifted her head in surprise. He'd always been sentimental, but the vulnerability in his voice felt new. It warmed her.

He continued, looking into her eyes. "Being with you is impossible to describe. You're the most intriguing woman I've ever met. I feel like the luckiest man in the world when I'm with you. I know that sounds corny."

Robin sighed. "I like corny."

"You amaze me just by being yourself," Matt said. His voice softened as he drifted toward sleep.

Robin watched him for a while as his breathing relaxed. She finally fell asleep around two in the morning.

At four, she woke to an empty bed. Startled, she sat up and heard the refrigerator door close. She slipped into her pink terrycloth robe and walked toward the kitchen.

Matt sat completely naked at the table eating a bowl of strawberries. Robin smirked.

"I was hungry," he said casually.

Robin shook her head in amusement and sat beside him. She took a strawberry and nibbled on it.

"I want you to know," Matt began as he looked at her, "this is the best date I've ever had."

"Well, I think every date we've had has been amazing," Robin replied.

He reached across the table and touched her cheek. She leaned into his hand.

"Matt," she said softly, "I know I don't always say much. And I know you wondered where you stood with me. I want you to know that I adore you. I love spending time with you. You make me feel safe. I can talk to you about anything."

"That goes both ways," he said, grabbing another strawberry. "I can't seem to get enough of you."

"Do you believe in destiny?" she asked.

"I didn't until I met you," he answered without hesitation. "I'm cautious by nature and I know you understand that. But what we have feels solid. It feels different."

"I'm glad we're on the same page."

"Oh yes, baby. I'm right there with you."

11

Matt and Robin spent the weekend together. Matt always kept an overnight bag in the trunk of his car in case he had to do a double at the hospital. They enjoyed every moment together. They watched movies, played cards, and explored their carnal desires repeatedly. By the time he left on Sunday morning, Robin was exhausted. It was still difficult to let him go. Wendy was right. The intimacy strengthened their bond.

Robin took some time during the week to self-reflect. She also spoke with her therapist. She summarized her interactions with Matt and explained how fond she was of him. She discussed some of her insecurities and concerns. Robin knew that Matt had unlocked a part of her that had been closed off. There was a soul connection to him. She knew she was falling in love.

The week passed by rather quickly. Matt invited Robin to his apartment on Friday night. She arrived and walked to the door. The screen door was open. Inside, Robin heard the gleeful yelps of a little girl. She smiled as she knocked on the aluminum screen door.

Matt came to the door with the little girl perched on his back. She had curly blonde pigtails and rosy cheeks. She was still laughing hysterically.

"Hey," Matt said breathlessly. "Wanna play?"

Robin smiled. "I didn't know this was your weekend with your daughter. I can go."

"Stop it. I invited you over knowing it was my weekend with her. Come inside," he beckoned as he turned and ran back into the apartment with the little girl squealing in delight.

Robin opened the door and let it gently shut behind her. She watched as the little girl slid off Matt's back and ran toward her. She stood confidently in front of Robin as she knelt down to eye level.

"I'm Olivia," she said sweetly as she offered her hand cordially.

"I'm Robin," she said as she shook Olivia's delicate hand. "It's very nice to meet you."

"My daddy calls me Olly, so you can, too."

"Oh okay. Well, it's a pleasure, Olly."

"My daddy said you were pretty." She had a wide smile and delicate, symmetrical features.

"Well, I think your daddy is pretty handsome, too," Robin said with a wink.

"I know. My mommy says that all the nurses think he's hot," she blurted out.

"Oh, I see," Robin acknowledged with a smirk.

Olivia ran off toward a room down the hall. Matt grinned wryly as he walked to Robin and kissed her lips softly.

"Hot, huh?" Robin said jokingly.

"Pssh... whatever," he said as he rolled his eyes.

"You thirsty?" he asked.

"If you have a bottled water, I'll take it," she replied.

He walked to the kitchen and emerged with a chilled bottle of water. He handed it to her and looked her over. "You're looking casually fine tonight. Do you have a boyfriend?" he asked humorously.

Robin looked down at herself. She was appreciative of the compliment, but she knew she didn't look that well put together. She wore a pair of white capri sweats, a red tank top, sneakers, and she pulled her hair up in a messy bun. Still, she appreciated the kind gesture. "Alas, I am taken." She laughed. "You look quite well yourself."

Matt had on a pair of army green shorts with a camouflage pattern and a black graphic t-shirt. He smiled and shrugged. "It's alright, I guess," he said.

Olivia walked into the living room. Matt immediately got her attention. He knelt before her. "So, I was thinking we could go rent some movies and play some putt-putt. Pizza for dinner at that place you love. What do ya think?"

"Yeah!" she shouted as she jumped up and down. "Can Robin come, too?"

"Absolutely!" Matt said with a beaming grin. "Can you go get your shoes on?"

"Yep!" she said as she turned and skipped down toward her room.

Robin pursed her lips. "She is beautiful, Matt."

"Thanks." He stood up and put his hands on his hips.

"You should've told me she was visiting this weekend. I feel like I'm imposing."

"Well, Sheryl and her husband are going away for the weekend, and I was more than happy to take her," he explained. "And you're not imposing. I wanted you to meet her."

"She's amazing," Robin said as she folded her arms.

Matt walked closer to Robin and kissed her lips softly. "So are you."

As Robin observed the interaction between Olivia and Matt during putt-putt, she couldn't help but miss her stepdad. He had taken her to putt-putt many times. He had always let her win, too. That's exactly what Matt was doing with Olivia. He missed simple putts to allow Olivia to move ahead with her score.

After putt-putt, they arrived at the pizza parlor. By 8:30 they settled back in at the apartment. After Olivia's bath, Matt popped in *The Wizard of Oz*. Matt sat in the rocker-recliner with Olivia. She quickly fell asleep. He finally excused himself and carried her to her room. Robin waited quietly on the couch. She heard the refrigerator door open. Matt emerged with a cold bottle of water. He handed it to her as he walked back to the recliner and sat down.

"If it's alright with you," Robin said as she loosened the bottle cap, "I'm going to head home in a bit. I don't want to leave a bad impression with Olivia."

"What do you mean?" he said with a faint scowl. His confusion was genuine, not irritated.

"Well, she's young and very impressionable. We're not married. I want to be consistent with the morals you're trying to instill in her."

"You don't have to go."

"The only way I'll stay is if you let me take the couch," she insisted.

Matt pursed his lips and nodded, thinking it through. "The couch it is." He took the bottle of beer off the end table and took a sip. "I really appreciate how considerate you are."

Robin nodded. "She's an amazing little girl, your Olly," she added.

"She is," he said with a long pause. He stared off into space for a moment and then added quietly, "Too bad she's not really mine."

"She isn't yours?" Robin asked. She remembered what Leah said about this being a possibility, but Robin hadn't pursued the topic.

"My marriage with Sheryl was very rocky. When things started to go south, we stopped being intimate. She cheated on me quite a few times. Then six years ago, she had an affair that would impact the rest of our lives. She got pregnant with Olly."

Robin listened intently. She saw the pain in Matt's face. "You did the right thing," Robin insisted.

"I believe that with my whole heart. I'm the one who walked the floors with her when she had colic. I'm the one who gave her baths and changed her. I don't give a damn who her biological father was. I am her dad. If I have anything to say about it, she'll never know otherwise."

"That is commendable, Matt."

"Believe me, I wanted to run far and fast." He shrugged, a small, honest gesture. "What can I say? I'm loyal."

"You're a good man," she said with a smile.

"Thank you," he said with a nod.

"Since we seem to be giving confessions tonight, I think I should tell you a little about my experiences. Maybe it will help you understand me a little better," Robin explained.

"Okay," Matt said as he moved from the recliner to the couch. He turned toward her and gave her his full attention, though he swallowed once as if bracing himself. "You can tell me anything, Robin."

"I met Brett Scott at a charity event. We were together for almost four years. The first two years were awesome. So, we moved in together. We lived together for about six months before the behavior began to shift. Brett had an addictive nature anyway, so I shouldn't have been surprised when he started using drugs. When he got high he just turned into someone different. That's common though, I'm sure you know that," she said as she began to tremble.

Matt reached for her hand. He wanted to provide as much comfort as he could, though his jaw tightened at the thought of anyone hurting her.

"Anyway," she said breathily, "he used to say really mean things. Mostly, it was about my weight."

"Your weight?" Matt asked, disbelief tightening his voice.

She nodded. "Yeah," she replied as she looked down at her hand in Matt's. "Brett became more and more violent. I didn't tell anyone. I always made excuses for him. What's worse is that I knew better. I knew what the cycle of violence looked like. I helped other people get out of it. I went to school to address these same kinds of problems. Yet, I couldn't pull myself out of it." She shook her head in disgust. Her eyes began to swell with tears. "One day he lost it. I mean, really lost it. He locked me in the apartment, and I thought for sure he was gonna kill me. Colin, do you remember him?"

"Yeah, yeah. The guy who works for the sheriff's department," Matt replied.

"Yeah. He played a direct part in getting me out of that shit safely," she nodded. She brushed tears from her cheeks and sniffled. "I blame myself. I should have been stronger. I should have left when the violence began, but I didn't. I stayed out of fear."

Matt exhaled slowly. "You can't carry all of this guilt," he said quietly. "Hindsight is 20/20. You can't change what happened. The guy was on drugs."

"I held out hope that he would get clean for me, but he didn't," she said as she pursed her lips.

"You rose from the ashes, Robin," he said softly, shaking his head a little.

She nodded and continued. "He is why I am so careful about who I let in. He cheated on me. He beat me. He abused me. I don't ever want to go through that again. That's why it's so hard for me to let my guard down."

Matt touched Robin's cheek and wiped away some of her tears. His expression tightened, a flicker of hurt on her behalf. "I will never raise a hand to you, Robin. I will also cherish you. I won't belittle you. You're such a good person. You're worthy of so much. You're entitled to be respected and loved. You know that, right?"

"I do now," she answered quietly.

Matt smiled, though his eyes were a little misty. He looked at Robin with intensity. "I really appreciate that you trusted me enough to share this with me. I'm glad you felt that you could confide in me." He brought her hand to his lips and kissed her palm. "I will never stop telling you how amazing you are. I promise you that you don't have to be scared anymore."

"I know." She still cried softly.

"Come here," he said as he pulled her into an embrace.

She wept softly as she relived the trauma. Matt leaned back onto the couch. Robin rested her head on his chest as she took some deep breaths. He kissed the top of her head.

"No matter what happens," Matt whispered, his voice wavering just slightly, "I will always be the one you can count on. When you're struggling, just tell me. I'll just love you harder. I will never give up on you."

His words caused a swell of emotion to flood from Robin. The reassurance she heard in Matt's voice and the sincerity of his words tore down what was left of her walls. She opened herself completely to whatever might happen between them.

12

Mid-August brought intense heat. School started again. Investigations were flooded with referrals. Robin was introduced to her new duties in a trial by fire. Still, she loved the opportunity to lead the department.

The softball season was coming to an end. There were only a few more games left. Robin was happy about this, too. She was looking forward to cooler weather.

It was Thursday. After her softball game, Robin drove back to her apartment for a nice, hot shower. As she made her way through town, she thought about all of the things she needed to do at work the next day. She also made a mental note of some personal budget items she needed to update. Tomorrow was payday, so she needed to make sure to put an extra payment on her student loans. The car payment for her new Jeep Grand Cherokee was also due.

As she pulled into the parking lot of the apartment building, she found her space and parked. An unfamiliar white Saturn sat a few spaces down.

Robin got out of her car and opened the back door. She grabbed some of her belongings out of the seat as she still eyed the Saturn. She knew every single car that was supposed to be in the parking lot of the apartment complex. The Saturn wasn't one of them.

She made her way onto the walkway and up the stairs. Sitting on a bench was a blonde woman. She was very stylishly dressed. She stood as Robin approached.

"You must be Robin," the woman said. Her voice was shrill and intense. "I could tell by the way Olivia described you."

Robin kept a poker face. "And you must be Sheryl."

"Yes," she replied. "I'm Sheryl Gregory."

"You mean Winston, right?"

"What?" Sheryl asked with venom in her tone.

"You aren't married to Matt anymore, so I'm assuming you misspoke." Before she could reply, Robin added, "Would you like to come in?"

"That won't be necessary," she said as she walked closer. "You need to quit seeing Matt."

Robin stayed composed as she listened.

"His daughter and I will always come first. You're not a mother, so I wouldn't expect you to understand."

Robin calmly inhaled and smiled serenely. She knew how to be diplomatic while also being assertive. "Let me explain something to you, Sheryl Winston. You have no control over me, Matt, or this situation."

"Oh, now see, that's where you're wrong. I have one thing you don't. I have his daughter."

"You think you can use Olivia as a gaming piece. You can't." Robin lowered her tone and locked eyes with Sheryl. "I know everything. I know that Olivia isn't biologically Matt's. I also know that because he is such a wonderful man, he stood by you and agreed to raise her as his own. Your manipulative tactics won't work this time. At least not with me," Robin assured her.

"How dare you!" Sheryl said as her face turned scarlet.

"Me?" Robin asked as she cocked her head. She was unable to be impassive any longer. She glared at Sheryl. "You come to my apartment to have a pissing contest? Maybe you don't understand exactly how divorce works. You gave up your rights when you set him free. If you thought for one minute you could intimidate me, you thought wrong. I'm not going to stop seeing Matt, and I will tell him about this. Grow up, Sheryl. Seriously." Robin concluded and walked past her. She opened the screen door and put the key in the lock. She twisted the knob and pushed the door open slightly.

Before she could exit the situation, Sheryl bit out, "He still loves me, you know?"

Robin stopped. She appeared frozen for a moment. She turned around slowly, her glare intensifying. "You think he still loves you?"

Sheryl put her chin up in a gesture of defiance. "Absolutely."

"I knew this day would come," Robin said quietly. "I knew you would exercise some sort of claim on him." She shook her head. "But here's how things are going to go, Sheryl. If you continue with this reckless behavior, if you continue to try to intimidate me by coming onto my property, I will have you arrested. Then I'll file a restraining order. So, by all means, keep going with this if you'd like to test me."

Robin turned on her heel, walked into the apartment, and closed the door behind her. She leaned against the solid safety of the door and caught her breath. Her heart pounded, and she closed her eyes for a moment to collect herself. Despite how cool she appeared during the interaction, the encounter still jolted her system.

Coming to herself, she put her bag on the floor and walked into the kitchen. Before she could put one foot onto the tile floor, her phone rang in her bag. She turned back and grabbed it. Matt's number came up on the screen. "Hello," she said.

"Did you tell my ex-wife off?" he asked without saying hello.

The question caught her off guard. It felt like Matt was preparing to defend her, but his tone held a flicker of exasperation that wasn't aimed at her. In the split second she had to process it, she felt her blood pressure rise as anger welled up inside of her. "Yes, I did," she answered curtly.

"Good," he said, letting out a breath. "It's about time someone put her in her place."

Relief swept over her. She closed her eyes as her shaking hands finally began to steady. "Really? You're not mad?"

"Hell no, I'm not mad," he said wryly. "I'm glad you did it."

"Glad? Why?"

"You're the first woman who hasn't been intimidated by her. She can be kind of terrifying," he admitted. "I figured she would scare you off."

"Not a chance," Robin said confidently.

"That's good," he laughed, the tension fading. "I guess it takes a little more than a pissed-off ex-wife to frighten you."

"You could say that," Robin said lightly.

"Well, I'm glad you didn't throw in the towel."

"Nope. It never even crossed my mind," Robin replied reassuringly.

13

The weekend arrived. Matt clocked out on Saturday morning, tired but grateful for the break. He got into his truck and drove toward Robin's apartment. He thought of her fondly; things were going well, better than he'd expected, honestly. He still felt lucky, almost cautious about it. They hadn't said those three little words yet. The timing just hadn't been right. Still, he knew he was falling in love with her.

Robin had given Matt an extra key to her apartment. They'd started taking turns staying with each other. When Robin stayed with Matt on weekends he had Olivia, she insisted on sleeping on the couch, determined to set a good example for his daughter. Her effort touched him more than he ever admitted out loud.

He pulled into the guest parking space beside Robin's car and made his way upstairs. The apartment was quiet as he moved down the hall into her room. She slept soundly, curled awkwardly toward the edge of the bed like she'd drifted off mid-thought. He untied his tennis shoes, slipped them off, stepped out of his jeans, and tugged off his T-shirt. He crawled into bed beside her and pulled her close. She stirred for only a moment before going still again. He kissed her shoulder, settled in, and let himself drift into sleep.

When he woke, Robin wasn't beside him. He heard the shower running. He got up, rubbed a hand over his face, and rummaged through the dresser drawer that held a handful of his things. He grabbed a pair of cotton shorts and put them on. As he walked into the hallway, he listened for Wendy and Terri, half expecting noise, but heard nothing. He assumed he and Robin had the apartment to themselves.

He knocked on the bathroom door to be sure Robin was the one showering. Her voice, warm but groggy, answered him. He walked in, slipped off the shorts, opened the glass shower door, and stepped inside.

Robin's back faced him as the water ran down her body. He was immediately aroused at the sight of her. He moved in and kissed her neck. When he touched her hip, he felt a different texture. He looked down. "You're wearing a birth control patch," he said, tracing it lightly with his finger.

"I've always worn one. I've just always made you wear a condom," she said, glancing over her shoulder.

"I don't mind wearing one if it makes you more comfortable."

"Well, I'm not making you wear one anymore," she said, her tone soft but teasing.

He touched her back and let his hands trail down her sides. "Is that so?"

Robin's skin warmed beneath his hands. "Matthew," she said, half-scolding, "we don't have time. We're already running late."

"I can be quick."

"I don't want you to be quick," she protested, turning to face him.

He smiled. "Neither do I, but we're definitely racing the clock here." His gaze drifted down her wet body. "You're absolutely breathtaking." His hands found her breasts, his voice low but earnest rather than polished.

Matt pulled her close and kissed her gently. He held her wrists and leaned in to kiss her neck, then worked his way to her collarbone. He heard her breathing change, not dramatically, just enough to know she was considering giving in.

He pressed her gently against the shower wall and lifted her leg. As he held her up, he pressed into her slowly. He kissed her deeply as she took him in. He moved with steady urgency. Holding her leg and tracing her skin with his free hand, he kissed her neck. "I love you," he whispered.

Robin pulled back slightly, surprise flickering before she grinned. "I love you, too."

He got lost in her eyes as he held her. The electricity between them could spook him at times, but he wanted it anyway. Her moans filled the shower as he felt her tighten around him. She released, and he followed soon after, a low sound of relief escaping him.

They let their foreheads rest together. "I do love you," Matt whispered, his voice rougher than he meant it to be.

Robin placed her hand on his cheek, her expression soft but real. "I love you, too."

14

Matt and Robin made the three-hour drive to the Hillard family cookout. They planned to stay with Robin's brother, Corbin, and his wife, Shelley. Richard, Robin's stepdad, and her mother, Amy, would finally meet Matt. Robin's younger sister, Maria, would also be participating in the get-together.

Corbin and Shelley had met in high school. Shelley had become more like a sister to Robin. She once had dark red hair, but over the years, it had lightened. She was still thin, and her skin was like porcelain. Her eyes were as blue as the ocean, although lately she complained she looked tired more often than not and blamed the kids for keeping her up at night.

Corbin was tall with dark hair and brown eyes. He was muscular from years of farming. He still ran the family farm and did most of the hard labor himself. Of course, he hired help, but he found fulfillment in what he did, even if he grumbled constantly about equipment breaking down, taxes climbing, and how nobody wanted to work anymore.

Robin stood in Corbin's kitchen stirring the potato salad. Shelley mixed up the pasta salad, wiping her hands on a dish towel every few seconds as if nervous or irritated. All of the others were outside by the in-ground pool.

"You look great," Shelley commented, though her tone hinted at a faint envy she didn't try very hard to hide.

Robin wore a black bikini with her hair pulled up. She smelled like suntan lotion. Her cheeks were the color of cherries from being out in the sun most of the day. "Aww. Thank you," she replied.

"You're glowing," she added.

"I feel great," Robin replied.

"Everyone seems to like Matt. He seems like a really great guy. And a doctor?" Shelley asked, her eyebrows lifting as if she wasn't sure how Robin had landed someone like that.

"He's not like anyone I've ever met before. He amazes me. He certainly caught me by surprise."

"I know that feeling," Shelley said in a melodic tone, though her smile faltered as if she'd thought better of the comment.

The front door opened and they heard Richard's voice. "Anyone home?" he called out with a southern drawl.

Richard had been a part of Robin's life since she was two. Shortly after she was born Robin's biological father died of cancer. Once her mother met Richard, they had quickly fallen in love. Wedding bells had followed, along with the occasional blended-family friction that came with the territory.

"We're in here," Shelley called out.

He walked in carrying a casserole dish covered with aluminum foil. The sunlight coming in through the patio door caught the silver in Richard's hair. His rosy cheeks always gave him a jolly appearance, though today he looked a little flushed from the heat and slightly out of breath from the walk in.

Robin walked to him and reached for the casserole dish. "Hey there daddy," she said.

"Ladybug," he said with a beaming smile. "Look at you! You look so good."

The compliment made her blush. "Where's mom?" she asked curiously as she put the casserole dish on the counter.

"She's coming with Maria," he answered. "They had to stop by the grocery store for a few more things." He looked around and shrugged. "So where's this feller you can't stop talkin' about?"

"He's outside with Corbin," she answered.

"Oh Lord. You didn't leave him out there with him, did you?" he joked, though a real concern lingered under the humor.

Robin smiled and looped her arm through Richard's. "Come on. I'll introduce you," she said as she led them out onto the patio.

Corbin and Matt's laughter carried through the air as they stood by the grill. Corbin slapped the side of it, muttering something about it acting up again and how nothing ever worked when he needed it to.

"Looks like they're getting' along just fine," Richard observed.

"Sure seems like it," Robin agreed. "Matt," she called.

He turned and walked to her. He wore a pair of khaki swimming trunks, his brown leather flip flops, and a white muscle shirt. "This is my dad, Richard."

Matt took off his aviator sunglasses and held out his hand to Richard. "Sir," he said with a nod. "It's great to meet you."

Richard chuckled as they shook hands. "Sir? Where'd you say this boy was from?" he said looking over at Robin. He turned his focus back to Matt again. "Son, you can just call me Rich."

Matt nodded, slightly embarrassed, glancing briefly at Robin as if unsure whether he'd already misstepped.

Within half an hour Amy and Maria arrived. Robin introduced them to Matt. They both showed sincere interest in him, though Amy's questions were a little too direct and Maria kept checking her phone between introductions, barely staying engaged. He quickly earned their respect, even if the process was a little clumsy.

Amy was an older version of Robin. She was still quite stunning even in her golden years. She had short hair, the dark color now gray. Her eyes were bright with some crows feet. She had laugh lines as well, signifying a joyful life well lived, but she also carried a heaviness at the corners of her mouth that suggested not every year had been easy. Her gaze lingered a little too long on Matt, as if trying to decide whether he was truly good enough for her daughter.

Maria was only a senior in high school. She had not been planned by Amy and Richard. Amy mistakenly thought she was through menopause. They took the surprise in stride and welcomed Maria in June eighteen years ago. Maria, however, often reminded them she hadn't asked to be the only child still at home and made sure everyone knew she was counting down the days until graduation.

The weekend of card games, board games, swimming, and relaxing on the deck gave Robin's family the opportunity to interact with Matt. He impressed them with his good manners and sincerity. His charming disposition won them over quickly, although Corbin teased him nonstop and seemed to be testing him more than befriending him, and Amy quizzed him a little too intensely about his career and future plans. By the time Robin and Matt left, the family was just as in love with Matt as Robin was, even if the road to that acceptance wasn't entirely smooth.

15

It was late September. The lazy Sunday was the perfect day for a picnic, so Matt and Robin ventured to the country. As they drove down a remote country road, a house appeared in the distance. It was large. Robin imagined how beautiful it must have been before it was abandoned, though a small pang of sadness hit her chest. Beautiful things didn't always stay beautiful. She knew that firsthand.

Suddenly, Matt pulled onto the lane leading to the house without warning. The land was overgrown. There were other homes nearby, but they were separated by a significant distance.

The large two-story white brick became more visible as they got closer. Truly, it was a wonder against the backdrop of the woods behind it.

"This place is absolutely amazing. Can you envision what it was like?" Robin said as she peered at it through the truck window. Her voice carried more excitement than she actually felt; she was partly filling silence, partly chasing her own curiosity.

"It's magnificent," Matt agreed, though a hint of tension sat in his voice.

Matt parked and turned off the engine. They stared up at the structure, awestruck by its size. Finally, Matt got out of the truck and grabbed the picnic basket out of the cab. Robin opened her door and hopped out. She took the blanket out of the back and shut the door, forcing a cheerful smile even though the abandoned house made her uneasy.

Quietly they sat on the blanket and ate. Robin took a drink of wine, still unable to take her eyes off the house. She tried to shake the strange sense of longing the place stirred in her. Then she felt

Matt's lips on her ear. Gently, he kissed her. Their sensual dance began as they made love under the tree on the soft plaid blanket.

Afterward, Robin rested in Matt's arms. She studied the home carefully. It was in severe disrepair. Still, the nostalgia of such a beautiful piece of the county's history was hard to ignore. A part of her liked imagining what had once been; another part feared what time could do to anything, including love.

"Come, love," Matt said. "Let's get dressed. I want you to see the rest of the property."

They dressed and walked toward the front of the house. Matt took her hand and led her inside. Robin looked up. She could easily see into the second floor through the holes in the floorboards. Her stomach tightened. This place was more than abandoned, it was unsafe. She bit back the instinct to comment.

"I want to buy it," Matt said, conviction edged with nerves. "And I want you to live in it with me."

She turned her head toward him. "What?" she asked. Her voice cracked. She was completely caught off guard, and her first instinct wasn't excitement but panic.

"You heard me. I want to be able to go to bed with you every single night and wake up with you every morning for the rest of my life."

Robin laughed once, too sharply, before softening it. Humor was her escape route. "But you sleep during the day, Vampire Man."

He smirked, but she saw he wasn't joking. The realization made her chest tighten.

"I want to marry you," he added.

She stopped breathing for a moment as his words registered. She pulled her hand away and turned to him. "Are you being serious?" she asked, her voice thin. She didn't handle surprises well, and this was the biggest one of her life.

"I want to have babies with you and grow old with you…"

His words washed over her, but instead of melting into romance, she froze. Babies. Marriage. Forever. The weight of it pressed into her ribs.

She was astonished. Immobilized by shock, she simply stood with her mouth agape. It wasn't graceful; it was fear taking the wheel.

"Marry me, Robin," he whispered, taking her hand again.

She finally broke her silence. "Matt, we've only known each other for a few months." Her voice trembled. "We don't even know if we can live together. I mean… what if we can't?" She hated how small and exposed she sounded.

"I know this is right."

"Matt, you haven't thought this through," Robin argued, but part of her knew she was projecting—she was the one who hadn't thought any of this through. Her heart raced. She chewed the inside of her cheek; a nervous habit she rarely let him see.

"I have thought it through. Do you have to think it through?"

She considered the question. She immediately knew the answer, but fear made her hesitate. She swallowed. "No. I don't have to think it through. I know how I feel about you." Her voice wavered with emotion and something else; vulnerability she couldn't hide.

Matt knelt down before her. Tears brimmed in her eyes. He pulled out a small velvet box from his jacket pocket. The lid stuck for a second before he opened it.

Robin's tears streamed down her face, but her smile wasn't perfect or serene. It trembled, caught somewhere between joy and terror.

"I know what you've been through," Matt said. "I know how hard it's been for you to trust me…"

Hearing that made her eyes drop. Trust had always been the tightrope she walked, never sure if she'd fall.

"I'm scared," she admitted. Her voice was barely a whisper, but it was honest, perhaps the most honest thing she'd said all day.

"I know you're afraid…"

"I have faith in us," she said with a nod, but she still wiped her palms on her jeans, grounding herself. She knew he was right. She also knew she was stepping into the unknown. "I'll marry you."

He stood and took her into his arms. He twirled around in a celebratory manner, nearly tripping on a loose board before laughing. She laughed too—high, nervous, relieved. He finally stopped and set her feet back on the floor. They sealed their decision with a kiss.

16

Matt stood at the nurse's station. He looked up at the clock on the wall. "Only 3 a.m.," he whispered to himself. He wearily rubbed his eyes. After tonight, he had three days off. A bed alarm chimed down the hallway, and someone called out for help with a combative patient. The ER felt louder than usual, or maybe he was just too tired to tune it out.

He continued noting encounters in the charts. Avery walked out of an exam room and stood beside Matt. "So, you're getting married," he commented.

The hint of negativity in his voice put Matt on the defense. His stomach tightened. "That's the plan," Matt replied as he continued looking through charts a little too intently, pretending he wasn't thrown off.

"Well, good luck with that buddy," Avery concluded with a pat on the back.

Matt shrugged, a little disappointed in his best friend. Avery and Matt had been through a lot. They had gone to high school together. They both knew they wanted to be doctors, so entering medical school together had been a no-brainer. It bothered him that Avery didn't sound happy for him, but he pushed the thought aside.

When Matt turned around to examine his next patient, he nearly ran right into Sheryl. Her appearance was startling. Her hair was messy, her eyes were red, and her scrubs looked like she had slept in them. "Is Olivia alright? It's the middle of the night."

"Yes, Matthew. She's fine. She's home with Kyle. Can I see you privately for a moment?" she asked.

He nodded and followed her into the doctor's lounge. A nurse walking past shot them a curious look. The overhead intercom buzzed with another page. Sheryl shut the door behind her a little too hard.

Matt sat down on the worn leather couch. He crossed one leg over the other, raised his arm, and put his hands behind his head. He laced his fingers together as he waited for Sheryl to speak. His foot bounced, betraying the exhaustion and anxiety he tried to hide.

She sat down beside him, desperation covering her face. "I'm begging you not to do this," she blurted out.

Matt lowered his arms and put his hands in his lap. He already felt his patience thinning. "What are you talking about, Sheryl?"

"It's all around the hospital that you asked Robin to marry you."

"Yes, I asked her to marry me. So what?"

"Don't do it. Please. I'm begging you."

"Why not?" he bit out. His voice cracked with irritation and fatigue.

"Matthew, I still love you. I want us to be a family."

Rage swelled within him as he stood up, but beneath it was a shaky exhaustion. "Jesus, Sheryl. You're such a player. It's the hunt you love, not me." The anger drew blood to his face. He scowled at Sheryl and folded his arms, taking a wide stance. His hands trembled slightly, though he forced them still. "I want you to listen to me. This is my shot at happiness, and I'm taking it. I have finally found someone that really loves me. She understands what it means to be a partner to me. You will never understand that because everything is always about you."

"Matthew, you haven't even known her that long. You can't possibly know that you're in love."

A monitor alarm beeped outside the room, adding to the pressure building in his head. The heat coursed through him as his heart pounded. "Let me see if I can get you to understand this. We met when we were juniors in high school. We got married when we were fucking kids. We stayed married for fourteen years. In all of that time, you never made me feel the way Robin does. She makes me feel heard. She allows me to have a voice, for fuck sake. She actually loves me. She shows me that she loves me. You never failed in making me feel like a complete disappointment. I was never enough for you. When you got pregnant with another man's child, I stayed. I stood by you because I made a commitment to us. I gave you some of the best years of my life. How could you possibly ask for more?"

"But what about Olly?" Sheryl said as she looked up at him. Her chin quivered in a way that looked practiced, not natural. She tried to appear weepy and vulnerable.

"Olivia loves Robin. You know she won't even sleep in the same bed with me when Olly stays. She says she respects me enough and respects the way I'm trying to raise her to avoid anything that would impede those efforts. She thinks of others, especially Olly. So stop dragging Olivia into this, Sheryl."

"If you love us you won't do this!" she shouted as she stood up defiantly. Her hands balled into shaking fists. She looked unstable, as if she could snap without warning.

"I've told you this repeatedly. I don't think you've heard me though." He paced, running a hand over his face. His breathing grew uneven, anger mixing with years of pent-up grief. "I will never break Olivia's heart by telling her that you slept with someone else and that she isn't mine. I will always take care of her. I love her. I always will. But you..." He trailed off again. His voice cracked. "I don't love you. I didn't even know what love was until I met Robin. She has taught me more about myself and about selflessness than anyone in my life ever has. I'm marrying Robin as soon as I can. That is final."

Sheryl suddenly rushed to him. She threw her arms around him and forcefully kissed him on the lip. Matt recoiled in shock. His hands flew forward and he shoved her away harder than he meant to.

"Stop this!" he exclaimed. His voice wavered with anger and fear. "Stop making a complete ass of yourself."

"We had something good Matt. Don't you remember?" Her voice pitched unnaturally high. Her smile twitched at the corners, unsteady.

"It wasn't good," he said, his voice higher and filled with annoyance. "I remember all of the nights that you didn't come home or when you came home smelling like another man. I remember feeling worthless because I always played the villain in your story. I remember hushed phone conversations. I remember that you had another man's child, Sheryl. It was impossible for you to stay faithful. So, what I remember is all of the hurt and the discontentment. You practically destroyed me."

Crocodile tears fell from her eyes as she struggled to harness genuine emotion. "I'm so sorry. I just know if we give it one more shot that we can make it work."

"You're delusional," he said as he threw his hands in the air. His voice shook with frustration. "Look, I'm not wasting my time with this anymore. I've got a job to do. I have patients to see."

He took a breath and began walking away, but then he stopped. He realized he needed to add a warning. Sheryl would be relentless in her efforts to destroy any happiness he had. He turned and walked back to her. His finger trembled as he pointed at her face. "I'm only going to say this once. You need to leave us alone. Stay away from us. The only time you need to contact me is when it involves Olivia. If you ever try to intimidate Robin again, or if you ever do this to me again, I will file menacing charges. I'm sick of your games. We're done, and I will not let you hurt Robin either. Do you understand me?"

Sheryl's expression twisted. Her eyes went cold and flat for a moment before filling again with forced tears. "You're going to regret this one day Matthew," she said through clenched teeth.

"The only thing I regret is ever meeting you." He turned abruptly and pulled the door open. The intercom overhead called a trauma to bay three. He walked out of Sheryl's life once more, though something deep inside him warned that she was not finished.

17

Robin moved out of her apartment and into Matt's at the beginning of October. They explained to Olivia their plans to get married. She was ecstatic. It soon became apparent that living together was already making things better between them.

They purchased the old country home in the middle of October. By the first week in November renovations began. Construction continued day and night. Matt and Charley started a lot of the work, and contractors were hired for other parts of the restoration. Everything was happening quickly, but nothing in their relationship had ever moved slowly.

Instead of pouring money into a large wedding, Robin and Matt decided to go before the justice of the peace. Their finances were better spent on the house. Neither of them wanted the stress of planning a big event when they were already juggling so many changes.

As they sat in the hallway of the courthouse, they waited patiently. Robin wore a pair of light-washed boot-cut jeans, a navy long-sleeved sweater, and brown loafers. Her hair lay in curls on her shoulders. Matt decided on darker boot-cut jeans, a gray graphic T-shirt, a gray sports jacket, and his Converse high tops. Their attire fit their personalities and the occasion perfectly.

They had already explained to their families that getting married at the courthouse wasn't about excluding anyone. It was simply practical. They hoped to host a gathering in the renovated home someday, but they weren't sure when that would be.

They were called into the court chambers and stood in front of one another. The secretary for the judge and a probation officer from juvenile court stood as witnesses. Robin and Matt held hands as the judge began discussing vows. Their eyes locked, and they got lost in one another. They had been waiting for each other their entire lives. It felt like their happy ending but also the beginning of everything new.

As they stood face to face, Robin remembered the freak accident that put her on Matt's path. She remembered his gentle touch and the sincerity in his eyes. She could hardly believe it had been less than a year.

Matt looked at Robin with appreciation and admiration. He had written off the possibility of marriage. He had given up. She changed his mind quickly, and he was thankful that she had. He was finally looking forward to the months and years ahead. He had found hope again.

The renovations and construction moved into December. Robin and Matt hoped they would be able to have Christmas in their newly remodeled home. Because things were moving so quickly, Christmas was a realistic goal.

One evening after work, Robin and Wendy met for an early dinner. Afterward, they made their way to the edge of town and into the country. The plan was to go to the house so Robin could get measurements for window treatments. Robin felt that familiar mix of excitement and tiredness that had followed her through the entire renovation process.

The outdoor layout of the house was simple. There were two entrances to the home. One faced the east side toward the large field. The other faced the west side toward the garage. The front entrance needed the most work. Instead of pouring sidewalks, large stones had been put down at the west side entrance. A sidewalk would eventually run from the main entrance to both the west and east sides.

An old oak tree stood on the other side of the garage. Gravel had been put down temporarily. When the weather warmed, concrete would go in with the rest of the walkways.

The east side entrance was covered by a porch with two sets of stairs leading off of it. Robin's grandmother's swing was stored in the garage but would be hung on the porch in the spring. Wooden rockers she had already purchased waited there as well.

Each entrance had new burgundy doors with white wooden screen doors. The windows were trimmed to match the doors and shutters.

The front entrance was aesthetic only. The west side would be used as the main entrance into the house. It was covered by a small overhang to protect the doorway from weather.

As Wendy and Robin walked through the west side door, they arrived in the kitchen. The flooring had already been restored to its original hardwood finish. Many planks throughout the house had been replaced, but everything matched well enough that most people wouldn't notice.

Robin paused, taking a moment to appreciate the progress. "It's finally starting to look like a home," she said quietly.

In the kitchen were two large windows looking out over the back of the property. They were trimmed in dark wood to match the baseboards throughout the home. All of the rooms were drywalled.

The kitchen connected to both the living room on the east side of the home and the large dining area on the north side. There were two ways to get to the dining room. The first was the kitchen. The second was through the hallway leading to the parlor on the east side, the staircase, and the front door.

Wendy stood in the living area. She walked to the fireplace which had been newly finished. "Is this original?" she asked in amazement.

Robin walked in behind her. "It is. Isn't it unique?"

"It's beautiful," Wendy said. She walked to the two large windows beside the east side door and peered out into the darkness. Lights glowed in the distance. "I take it those are your closest neighbors?"

Robin nodded. "I believe so. Let me show you the rest."

They walked out of the living room and back into the kitchen. Robin led Wendy down the hallway. She pulled open a set of pocket doors to reveal the parlor. It was small compared to the dining area and living room. Charley and Matt had restored the original fireplace there, too. Two windows looked out over the east and north sides of the property. A set of double-decker closets covered the entire south wall with the fireplace in the middle.

"Look at the tapestry on these walls," Wendy said as she touched the west wall. "You were able to restore this?"

"I found something similar to the original, so we updated it a little," Robin explained. "Want to see the upstairs?"

"Of course I do."

They walked to the enclosed stairwell leading to the second floor. The small landing held a round window facing the west side of the property.

"I can't believe you were able to keep these either," Wendy said as she looked down at the stairs.

"That wasn't easy," Robin said. "Most were in bad shape. The ones that still creak, those are the originals. Not many though."

Upstairs, Robin led Wendy into the master bedroom. Two floor-length windows faced the front of the property. Another restored fireplace sat along the west wall. Old double-decker closets filled that wall as well.

Wendy looked up at the newly plastered ceiling and modern light fixtures. "Did all the wiring have to be replaced?"

"Oh yes. The home wasn't up to code at all. Charley's friend came in and did everything. Let me show you Olly's room."

The window there was much smaller but suited the space. The fireplace was in the process of being torn out. They planned to build a closet in its place. Wendy nodded approvingly.

Robin led her back into the hallway and opened a set of double doors. "The linen closet."

Wendy nodded.

Robin pointed toward the bathroom. "Everything in there had to be completely overhauled. It was a disaster." She pointed to a room across the hall. "That's going to be a study. It's the same size as the master, which was nice."

"A nursery someday maybe?" Wendy teased.

"Maybe," Robin replied softly. She wasn't ready to go there yet.

They went back downstairs and entered the basement. Robin pointed as she explained where everything would go. Wendy listened with genuine interest.

"Are you putting this place on the registry?" Wendy asked.

"Yes. Because we're restoring instead of rebuilding, we think it'll be approved. The State may reimburse some of the renovation. I want to research the home's origins, but I don't have time right now."

"So, we're measuring the windows tonight?" Wendy asked.

"Yes. I need to get the window treatments ordered."

They walked back upstairs. Robin handed Wendy a pencil and paper, grabbed a ladder, and moved it to the master bedroom. She climbed the ladder and began calling out numbers as Wendy wrote.

A slamming door downstairs startled both of them. Robin's stomach tightened, but she forced herself to stay calm. "It's probably just Charley. He works all hours," she said lightly. "We're up here," she called out.

Silence answered her.

"Did you leave one of the doors open?" Wendy asked, her tone edged with worry.

"I think I did," Robin said, though she couldn't remember.

The tension was almost tangible as they looked at one another. Robin's pulse quickened.

She climbed down the ladder and walked to the doorway. She checked the upstairs rooms first. Nothing was out of place. Nothing felt disturbed.

Unarmed and unprepared, Robin made her way down the stairs. Wendy followed cautiously. They checked every room, including the basement. No intruder. No contractor. No Charley.

Robin stood in the kitchen with a perplexed expression. She shrugged. "I must have left the east or west entrance open. Wind must have caught it."

"Must have," Wendy echoed, though her eyes revealed doubt.

18

By mid-December the restoration and renovations were nearly complete. The decorating process began. Robin and Matt took the month off to focus entirely on finishing the house. They decided to stay there so they could work from the time they woke until the time they went to sleep, though living inside an active renovation quickly proved to be less romantic than they had imagined.

The kitchen painting took a full day. The beige valances against the burgundy walls gave the space a modern appearance. The island and matching countertops finally arrived, so Robin and Matt focused on installing those. Matt muttered under his breath more than once when a screw refused to line up or the drill slipped in his hand. He installed a copper pot rack that hung from the ceiling above the island. The new stainless-steel appliances arrived soon after.

Robin and Matt painted the living room a dark shade of taupe. The dining room became a sage green with white trim. The parlor was a light beige, the tapestry on the west wall featuring browns and burgundies. The closet doors in the parlor were painted white. Robin kept stepping back to assess her work, sometimes sighing when she noticed uneven edges she had to redo.

She found a long oak table with a matching bench and chairs for the dining room on an antique site. She ordered it, and it was delivered during their time off.

Robin painted the master bedroom in a rich brown while Matt painted an accent wall in the study in navy blue. He accidentally streaked a section of the ceiling and swore softly before touching it up. Robin placed an electric accent candle in each window. The ivory-colored ruffled curtains arrived for the study, master bedroom, dining room, parlor, and living room. For the bathroom, she chose light yellow valances and painted the walls white. As a final touch, she stenciled daisies along the upper border, though she had to redo one row after she smudged a petal with her thumb.

Before the claw foot tub could be restored and delivered, Matt installed tile in the bathroom. The hardwood floor beneath it had been too damaged to save, and Charley had reinforced the subfloor once the old boards were ripped out. Matt kept complaining about his knees hurting from being on the tile floor all day.

Robin and Matt agreed on a primitive theme throughout the home, believing it honored the house's origins. Olivia's room was the exception. Robin wanted to surprise her with a Super Girl themed bedroom. She chose red curtains and painted two walls, hero blue and the other two white. On one white wall, she painted a comic style mural of Super Girl. A large shaggy red rug lay in the center of the room to complement Olivia's new white furniture. Matt stepped in midway through the mural and said, "Her left arm looks longer than the right," which earned him a sharp look from Robin as she told him gently but firmly to hush.

As Robin stood on the ladder finishing one of the mural scenes, she saw Matt in her peripheral vision. He leaned against the doorframe wearing old gray sweats, work boots, and a torn shirt. He was covered in paint and sawdust. His hair stuck up in places from running his hands through it too many times.

"My God, you're hot," he said.

She looked down at herself. She wore red sweatpants, flip flops, and a tie-dyed shirt. Paint decorated her arms and streaked through her ponytail. She felt grimy and desperately needed a shower. "Well, I'll tell you, Dr. Gregory," she said as she turned back to the wall, "I do not feel hot."

"Since we're still waiting on furnace parts, I tried the fireplace in the living room."

"Oh. No more space heaters?"

"No more space heaters," he said, folding his arms and nodding with exaggerated confidence. "I'll get the other two fireplaces going tomorrow if I need to."

"Well, the house is still standing, so the fireplace must be working pretty well," Robin joked.

"Why don't you come down off that ladder and call it a night?" he asked, stepping farther into the room.

She agreed. Her back ached and her hands were stiff from painting.

Suddenly, the door from the kitchen to the basement slammed. Robin climbed down from the ladder and looked at Matt. He looked equally confused, brows pulling together.

"Do you think Charley would be here this late?" he asked.

She shrugged.

"You're a cockblock, Charley," Matt called out. "We're upstairs."

They waited for his reply but heard nothing. A moment later, they heard footsteps coming up the stairs. Matt stepped into the hallway. Robin followed. Both expected to see Charley appear.

No one did.

"Stay here," Matt whispered. He went to the study and retrieved his gun. He moved down the stairs and into the kitchen. Robin waited, her pulse thudding in her ears. The memory of the slammed door during her visit with Wendy returned sharply.

"It's safe," Matt called. "It's just you and me."

Robin walked down the stairs and saw him standing in the living room. He shrugged. "No one's here but us."

The look on her face made it clear that his explanation did not satisfy her.

"Honey, this house is old. Nothing is square. These doors are going to shift and shut on their own. A draft catches them and there you go," he said, though his voice lacked its usual confidence.

"It doesn't make sense," she argued. "The doors are brand new."

Matt had no answer.

"This same thing happened to Wendy and me when we were measuring windows," she added.

"What happened?"

"A door slammed. No one was here but us."

He shook his head. "We're just tired. It's a new place. It's old."

His explanation was reasonable, but Robin did not entirely believe it. Still, when he took her hand and led her into the living room, she let her worry settle into the background. He had laid out a comforter and a couple of pillows on the floor.

"Come lie down with me," he said as he began undressing.

She pushed aside her unease and undressed as well. She joined Matt on the comforter. He pulled a second blanket over them as they rested their heads on the pillows. They faced one another, and his palm fit naturally along the curve of her waist.

"I love you," he whispered.

"I love you too," she said.

"This is just the beginning for us. We're breathing new life into this old place."

"I know," she said, running her fingers through his hair, feeling paint flakes brush against her skin.

The glow of the fire reflected in their eyes, intensifying the heat between them. They made love, officially christening the room in the old house.

19

Although work continued on little things in the house, everything was mostly finished. Robin and Matt prepared to celebrate their first Christmas together. They put up a tree in the living room and in the parlor. The house was decorated with lights, and the mantles were adorned with fresh pine from the trees in the woods near the back of the property. Stockings hung from the living room fireplace.

Robin and Matt eagerly awaited Olivia's arrival. She hadn't yet been to the house. Robin sat in the parlor looking out at the east field while working on her laptop. She took a drink of hot chocolate and set it back on the small rectangular table beside one of the burgundy wingback chairs. She heard the kitchen door slam. Startled and apprehensive, she froze, her heart jumping before she reminded herself that they were expecting Olivia. Then she heard Olivia's voice.

"Robin!" she shouted.

Relieved, Robin let out a breath she hadn't realized she was holding. She closed her laptop quickly, almost too quickly, and fumbled it slightly before steadying it with her other hand. She placed it on the large desk in the parlor and walked out into the hallway. Olivia stood in the kitchen still bundled in her pink parka and knit hat, glowing with excitement.

Robin walked in and held out her arms. She embraced Olivia and kissed her cheek. "Happy Christmas!" she said gleefully. "Oh, you look so good I think I'll eat you up!"

Olivia giggled as Robin made munching noises against her neck. "Let me take your coat and hat," Robin said as she unzipped her coat.

"This place is so big!" Olivia exclaimed as she pulled one arm out of the sleeve.

Robin smiled, brushing a stray pine needle off her sweater. She had been decorating all morning and hadn't noticed it stuck there.

"Hey, who lives next door?" Olivia asked. "They have a Santa on their lawn."

"That's Mr. and Mrs. O'Bryan's place," Matt answered as he walked in. He closed the door with his hip because his hands were full, one holding his gloves, the other still gripping a tape measure he had forgotten to set down. Snow clung to the bottom of his jeans. "They have grandkids I know you'll want to meet."

"They've lived there for a really long time," Robin added.

Once freed from the coat, Olivia went to work removing her snow boots. She held them up as melting snow pooled into a small puddle at her feet.

"Take them over to the boot tray, please," Robin said.

Olivia did as she was asked and, without prompting, tore off a paper towel and handed it to Robin. Robin smiled, bent down, and sopped up the puddle. As she stood, her knee cracked loudly, loud enough for Matt to glance over. She pretended not to notice. "Can you toss this in the garbage can for me?" she asked.

Olivia nodded and tossed the soiled towel. "Where's my room?" she asked excitedly.

"Come on. We'll show you," Matt said, leading the way. Olivia followed energetically, anything but timid, while Robin trailed behind, smoothing her hair self-consciously. She had checked that room ten times already and still worried she had missed something.

When they reached the top of the stairs, Matt said, "Close your eyes." Olivia squeezed them shut dramatically. Matt guided her toward the room, nearly stepping on one of her dropped boot socks in the hallway. He muttered, "Whoops. Hazards," and nudged it aside with his foot.

Robin stepped in front, opened the door, and moved aside. Matt let go of Olivia's shoulders. "Open your eyes."

Her eyes flew open. Her mouth dropped. She squealed and jumped up and down, clapping wildly. "Super Girl! I love it!" She ran to Matt and leapt into his arms, knocking him slightly off balance so he had to take a quick step back to steady himself.

"Don't thank me, Munchkin. Thank Robin. She picked everything out and did the mural," Matt said, still catching his breath.

Olivia hopped down and approached Robin. She knelt in front of her and smiled widely.

"Thank you. I love it. I can't believe you did all of this for me."

"You're very welcome. You said you wanted Super Girl," Robin said with a playful shrug. Inside, she felt a swell of relief. She had worried all week that the mural wasn't good enough.

"But I didn't think you'd do it," Olivia said. "Mommy told me it would just be too hard."

Robin felt a flash of irritation at Sheryl's comment, but she swallowed it and kept her voice gentle. "Olly, nothing is too hard for you. Nothing." She touched her cheek and kissed her forehead. "Want to go see the basement? There's stuff down there for you, too."

"Yeah!" Olivia shouted.

Matt was already downstairs when they arrived. He had clearly rushed; his shirt was slightly untucked on one side, and he smoothed it down when he saw Robin notice. Along the west wall were the washer and dryer and utility sink. The water heater, furnace, and electrical boxes were also there. In the middle of the room was a long folding table. Cabinets lined the east wall. An extra bathroom stood enclosed in drywall.

Where framing had once stood was now more drywall and a closed wooden door. Matt opened it, bumping the doorstop lightly because he forgot how fast it swung. He let Olivia in first.

The room was painted light pink. Butterflies stenciled by Robin danced across the walls. Cream-colored Berber carpet covered the floor. A large dollhouse sat in one corner. A toy box and walk-in closet overflowed with more toys.

"You get your own playroom," Matt said.

Olivia grabbed a stuffed animal and hugged it tightly. "Thank you so much!"

For Robin, everything she had done, every late night, every splinter, every paint smudge on her skin, had been worth it. Seeing Olivia this joyful made her eyes sting. She blinked the feeling away before Matt noticed.

Robin helped Olivia settle into her room, then gave her a bath and got her into pajamas. Olivia stayed upstairs playing while Robin returned to the kitchen to load the dishwasher. Matt stayed in the study, though at one point she heard him sneeze loudly, and Olivia burst into laughter. Then came the thumping of footsteps in the hallway overhead.

Robin smiled. She couldn't be happier with how the house had turned out. And Olivia, happy, loud, thriving, made it all feel complete. As she cleaned the countertops, she reflected on the last few months. It was hard to grasp where the year had begun and how it was ending. The journey had been so quick.

Matt walked into the kitchen, smiling with tired eyes. He shoved his hands into his jeans pockets, then pulled one out again when he realized he was still holding a tiny pink hair tie Olivia must have handed him. "She wants you to tuck her in," he said.

"Really?"

"That's what she said."

It was the first time Olivia had asked for Robin at bedtime. Robin placed the towel on the counter, her stomach flipping with nervous joy.

She walked upstairs into Olivia's room. Olivia sat on the bed flipping through a picture book.

"What are you reading?" Robin asked, sitting beside her.

"Oh, Daddy just read me *Green Eggs and Ham*. It's my favorite."

"I liked that book, too." Robin paused, studying Olivia's little face and feeling grateful for the chance to become her stepmom. "You ready to lay down?"

Olivia nodded and handed her the book. Robin stood, returned it to the white bookshelf, and came back. Olivia snuggled beneath the covers, and Robin pulled the red down comforter under her arms.

"Love you, dear heart," Robin said, kissing her forehead.

"Love you, too," Olivia whispered with a contented exhale. "I just wanted you to tuck me in."

"Well, I'm glad you did," Robin said, cheeks warm.

"Good night, Robin," Olivia said as she turned toward the wall.

Robin smiled. "Night, sweetie," she whispered, pulling the door shut.

20

A warm bath sounded like heaven as Robin grabbed a towel from the linen closet. She went into the bathroom, plugged the tub, and turned on the water.

She made her way to the master bedroom, grabbed a pair of cotton pajamas from the antique dresser, and walked back to the bathroom. The sound of water hitting porcelain, paired with the crackling fire down the hall, was soothing.

Robin laid the towels on the toilet, pushed the door mostly closed, and hung the pajamas on the back hook. She turned to the pedestal sink, ran the hot water, and cleaned the makeup from her face.

She reached into the medicine cabinet for essential oils and poured a few drops into the bathwater. Vanilla and lavender filled the room. She closed her eyes, letting the scent settle her.

She undressed, tossing her clothes into the white wicker hamper. The soft yellow bathmat warmed her feet. After lighting a few candles on the back of the toilet, she stepped into the tub and lowered herself into the water.

She rested her head on the bath pillow. The muffled television murmured downstairs. Then she heard it… giggling in the hallway. Her eyes opened. The bathroom door sat nearly closed, blocking her view.

"Olly?" Robin called.

No answer.

She exhaled and sank back again. Olivia probably didn't want to get in trouble.

But then the giggling came again, lighter this time, almost playful. A sudden chill swept over Robin's skin, raising the fine hairs along her arms. She sat up.

"Olly, you need to go to bed," she called, more firmly.

Silence.

Robin stood, water cascading back into the tub. She wrapped herself in her robe and stepped onto the rug. Opening the bathroom door quietly, she peered into the dim hallway. Only the glow from the bedroom fire lit the space, and the air felt noticeably colder than before.

She walked to Olivia's room and eased the door open. Olivia slept soundly, curled around her stuffed animal.

Robin turned back toward the bathroom. The giggle floated through the hallway again, faint yet unmistakable.

A prickling sensation ran up her spine. She stepped into Olivia's room once more. The child hadn't moved an inch.

Trying to steady her breathing, Robin hurried downstairs instead of returning to the bath.

Matt sat by the fireplace wrapping presents while the television flickered in the background. Her terrified expression caught him immediately.

He stood and walked to her, placing his hands on her shoulders. "Robin, what's wrong? You look shaken."

Her voice wavered. "I was taking a bath and heard giggling. I thought it was Olly, but she was asleep. I stepped into the hall and heard it again. Matt, I don't want to go back up there alone."

He softened. "Sweetheart, it's probably just the TV echoing upstairs, or Olly talking in her sleep. Sound carries weird in this house."

"Matthew, it wasn't her." Robin's hands trembled.

"I'll go with you," he said gently. "Your bathwater's probably cold. Let's warm it up and try again. I need to put laundry away anyway."

Robin nodded.

They returned upstairs. Robin let out some of the cooled bathwater and turned on the hot faucet while Matt placed towels in the linen closet, moving with calm, deliberate motions.

When the water warmed, she hung up her robe and stepped in again. Steam rose around her. Matt finished his tasks and sat on the closed toilet lid, watching her quietly for a moment.

"You've had a lot going on," he said. "The move. The promotion. The holidays. Anyone would be overwhelmed."

"You think I imagined it?" Robin asked.

"I'm saying it's possible," he replied carefully. "I trust what I can touch and measure. Most things have logical explanations."

Robin's brows drew together. "You don't think it could be real? Do you believe in anything beyond what we see?"

He hesitated. "I believe this life is what we have. I haven't seen anything that proves otherwise."

"So no higher power? No guidance? Nothing outside ourselves?"

He brushed a hand through his hair. "I've never seen God. Have you?"

"I'm not only talking about God," Robin said softly. "I mean a creator. A higher source. Something beyond us."

He leaned his elbows on his knees. "I think we're biology. Chemicals firing, bones moving, nerves reacting. We live, we die, and we feel things in between. That's the extent of it."

His tone wasn't unkind, but it was unwavering. A man shaped by too much hard truth.

Robin felt her chest tighten. "So, no afterlife? No miracles? Nothing unseen?"

Matt's voice was quiet but pained. "I've watched children die for no reason. Good people suffer horribly. Where is divinity then? Where was it when you were held hostage?"

The words struck her. She looked down, gathering herself. When she finally spoke, her voice was barely above a whisper. "I wasn't alone."

He didn't hear her. "Life hurts because it's just… life. Nothing mystical about it."

Robin steadied her breath. "My stepdad was a Pentecostal preacher. My siblings and I hated church, but there were moments we felt things we couldn't explain. I learned early that religion and spirituality aren't the same. Religion confines. Spirituality frees."

She paused. Sharing the next part felt vulnerable, but she went on.

"When Brett almost killed me, I felt a peace I couldn't explain. Like someone was with me. After that, I searched for meaning. Spirituality helped me heal in ways religion never could."

Matt's expression softened a little. "So, you don't believe in God the way you were taught."

"I believe in a higher source. Something loving. Something guiding. I was raised to fear God, not understand him. Fear is control. Spirituality is growth."

"What about Jesus?" he asked quietly.

"I believe Jesus was divine. Maybe the Creator in human form."

"And the Bible?"

"I see it as a collection of stories written long after Jesus lived. There's truth in it, but I think all religions hold pieces of truth. We're meant to find what resonates."

"And angels?"

"They're spirit guides. Some human, some not. They protect and guide us."

Matt rubbed the back of his neck. "How have we never talked about this?"

"I don't know. It just didn't come up."

He stood slowly. "I'm going to finish in the bedroom."

Robin watched him walk away. Her heart felt heavy. She tried not to take his disbelief personally, but the divide between them felt wider than she expected.

As she sank deeper into the water, a quiet ache settled beneath her ribs. Something had shifted, subtle yet unmistakable, and she wasn't sure how to stop it from widening further.

21

Christmas morning arrived. Because of the investment in the house, Robin and Matt decided to focus on Olivia's gifts. They explained their situation to their families, and everyone was understanding and supportive.

After Olivia opened her gifts, she retreated to the playroom in the basement. Matt and Robin snuggled together on the couch as the flames blazed in the fireplace. Christmas music echoed throughout the space. The colored lights on the tree made everything sparkle.

Matt looked down at Robin with a small smirk tugging at his lips.

"What?" she asked curiously. "What are you smiling about?"

"I have a gift for you," he said.

Robin's stomach dipped. "Matt, we agreed not to buy each other gifts."

"I know. But it's our first Christmas." His tone was light, but she felt something underneath it. A hopefulness. Maybe even a need to make things right after the night before.

"Matthew," she said softly, half-scolding, half-worried. She didn't want to disappoint him again.

He broke their embrace and stood. "Just wait here." He disappeared into the hallway. Robin smoothed her pajama pants, suddenly nervous. She hoped this wasn't another moment where they missed each other emotionally.

He returned carrying a large square box. He sat beside her, expression bright but fragile at the edges, and placed the box carefully in her lap.

"Matt, what did you do?" she asked, her voice almost a warning.

"Just open it," he said, though his fingers tapped anxiously on his thigh.

She opened the lid. Inside was a straw hat with a wide white ribbon. She blinked at it, unsure of its meaning, and raised one eyebrow at him.

He took a slow breath. "I wanted to talk to you before I actually booked anything. We said no honeymoon because of the house, but I don't want us to skip it. I think we should go on a trip."

"A trip?" she repeated, surprised.

"Yes. A cruise."

Robin's chest tightened. The timing, the money, her job, all of it felt heavy. "Matt, all of our money is tied up until the house is put on the registry."

"Not all of it," he said quickly. "I've been putting money back, and I talked to a travel agent. We could go in the fall. Five days. From Miami. It would be something for us. Something to look forward to."

She smiled, but it wavered. She glanced back into the box and then at him. "It sounds lovely, but..." She trailed off, trying to find the right words.

He leaned forward. "You know it would be good for us. For you."

That pierced her more than she expected. After their conversation the night before, she wondered if he thought a trip would smooth things over.

"I appreciate the thought," she said gently. "I do. But I don't think we can."

"It wouldn't be until fall. And I'm paying for it."

"It isn't about the money." She hesitated. "With my job, I really need to stay close right now."

His shoulders fell. The disappointment crossed his face openly before he tried to hide it. "It's months away," he murmured.

"I've hurt your feelings," she said softly.

"No," he said, shaking his head, though his voice lacked conviction.

Robin shifted closer. "Matt, can I say something?"

He nodded. His eyes remained downcast.

"We're really terrible at pretending we're fine when we're not. I can tell when you're shutting down. And I don't ever want you to feel like you can't tell me what you're feeling, even if it isn't what I want to hear."

He let out a breath, the kind that carried more weight than sound. "I just wanted to give you something special," he admitted. "I didn't get to give you a honeymoon. I don't want you to feel like I failed you."

Her heart softened. She touched his hand. "You haven't failed me. Not even close. We have each other, and that's more important than any trip. The idea is beautiful. I just don't think the timing is right. Not with everything going on."

He looked at her, searching her face for reassurance. "Just promise me that someday you'll let me take you. I don't want you to feel cheated."

Robin smiled warmly and squeezed his hand. "There is no possible way I could ever feel cheated."

But even as she spoke, a small worry flickered in her chest. It was a quiet hope that they weren't beginning a pattern of wanting different things at different times.

22

After an enjoyable three weeks off, Matt and Robin returned to their respective jobs. The snow made the commutes difficult, but the joy of coming home to a cozy house was worth it.

For Robin, however, the house still made her uncomfortable at times. There were moments she felt as if she were being watched. In spite of her steadfast faith, she often felt on edge. She began working late and sometimes to the point of exhaustion. She even started going out on calls with the investigators she supervised just to avoid being alone in the house. When that didn't ease her nerves, she made dinner for Matt and took it to the hospital, then slept in the on-call lounge. She knew none of these were permanent solutions.

Something about the house wasn't right. The earlier incidents hadn't faded from her mind, and they contributed to her constant unease in the newly remodeled space. They reminded her of things she had experienced in childhood. She wasn't ready to share any of that with Matt, especially after he revealed his skepticism. With Matt gone most nights, the house felt larger, emptier, and harder to rationalize.

Eventually, Wendy offered to stay with her. She slept over occasionally, but that wasn't sustainable either. Robin also didn't want to intrude on Terri and Wendy's relationship.

As time passed, Matt's midnight shifts began taking a toll on the marriage. Robin kept her dissatisfaction and trepidation to herself. She knew how hypocritical this was, especially after their Christmas conversation about communication.

Eventually, Robin decided to adopt a dog from the local shelter. Matt didn't object. He knew something was deeply wrong, and he hoped a dog would give Robin companionship and help her feel more secure in their home.

Cookie was a mutt covered in golden, shaggy fur. He was rather large for a five-month-old pup. Robin used crate training for potty training and kept the crate in the basement so any accidents wouldn't damage the new flooring. Cookie was rarely alone. When Robin worked, Matt was home, and vice versa.

Months went by with no strange occurrences. The snow melted into spring. Soon the trees were budding, and the March rains began. By then, Cookie was completely potty trained and slept on a dog bed in the master bedroom beneath one of the large windows.

A spring storm blew through as Robin watched television in the living room. As she rested on the couch, she drifted off. Suddenly, a crash of thunder shattered her slumber. She shot upright, startled and shaken. She glanced at the grandfather clock as it chimed once. Cookie, who had been lying at her feet, perked up as the thunder rolled.

Once she caught her breath, Robin lay back down and pulled the blanket over her shoulders. The television played quietly. Cookie burrowed under the blanket and settled on Robin's bare feet, groaning as he got comfortable.

Another loud noise came from upstairs. It echoed through the house. A door slammed above her, and she heard heavy footsteps on the stairs. She wondered if Matt had come home early, saw her asleep, and decided not to wake her. Maybe he was going upstairs for a shower.

The door slammed again. Cookie jumped off the couch and barked loudly. Robin tried to remain logical, but she called out for Matt anyway. When he didn't answer, her heart pounded and adrenaline rushed through her veins.

She got up and walked into the parlor. She grabbed a ball bat from the closet and held it tightly. Slowly and deliberately, she started up the stairs. The wooden planks creaked beneath her bare feet, and Cookie followed closely behind.

When she reached the landing, she saw the soft glow of the decorative lamp on the hallway table. With the bat raised, she continued up and switched on the light at the top of the staircase. Cookie moved past her and trotted down the hallway toward the bathroom.

Robin stood at the top of the stairs assessing the situation. Nothing seemed out of place. All of the doors were open. To be certain, she moved from room to room, switching on lights and checking closets. Cookie stayed close as she made her inspection.

After one final look around, Robin decided to go downstairs to turn off the television. She lowered the bat and shifted her weight to head back down. Realizing Cookie wasn't beside her, she turned to see him standing in the middle of the hallway, growling at the bathroom doorway. The hair on his back stood straight up. He lowered his head as if preparing to attack. Then he urinated on the floor, baring his teeth.

A brief flash of irritation cut through her fear. Cleaning up the mess was something she could control, unlike whatever was happening in the house.

She walked toward the bathroom, grabbed toilet paper, and returned to clean up the puddle. Cookie continued barking.

"Cookie," she said gruffly. "That's enough."

Robin stood and carried the soiled toilet paper to the bathroom. After tossing it into the toilet, she walked toward the staircase again. A cold chill washed over her. She turned.

A formless light drifted across the hallway and disappeared into the study. A giggle followed from the room. Robin watched as Cookie's demeanor changed. He relaxed, sat down, and wagged his tail, as if the air itself had shifted.

Then a whisper brushed her ear. "Help us."

The hair on her neck rose. Goosebumps covered her arms. Her breath came shallow. She turned slowly, expecting someone to be behind her, but she stood alone with her dog.

Cookie's behavior shifted again. He rose and became more aggressive. Robin felt like they were both caught on some emotional roller coaster. An overwhelming sadness settled on her, heavy and almost foreign, and tears spilled down her cheeks. A cold hand touched her arm.

"Help us, please," the voice pleaded again. This time the sorrow in it felt too deep to belong to anything living.

"I don't know how," Robin whispered.

The cold sensation lifted. She tried to collect herself and finally walked downstairs into the living room. She called for Cookie, who hadn't followed.

"Cookie, come."

She waited for the sound of his nails on the floor.

"Cookie, come now!" she shouted. At last he obeyed, scurrying into the room.

After turning off the lights and the television, Robin reluctantly walked back upstairs with Cookie close behind. Exhaustion overwhelmed her. Sleep had been slipping from her grasp for weeks, leaving her raw and frayed. She tried to push the incidents out of her mind as she crawled under the covers. Cookie settled onto his dog bed. Robin reached over and turned off the lamp on the nightstand.

She finally drifted off to sleep once more.

23

"Robin, help me, please," a voice called out to her.

Robin drifted somewhere between consciousness and sleep. Again, she heard the soft voice. "Robin." She startled awake and looked around the room. No one was there. Cookie rested peacefully on his bed. She turned to the nightstand. The red numbers on the clock read 5:30.

She settled back down, convincing herself she must have been dreaming. She drifted off again. Suddenly, a violent tug yanked her ankle, and a deep voice echoed through the room. "You can't help them."

Her eyes flew open. She jerked her foot away and screamed. Her hands shook as she reached for the lamp and switched it on. The commotion caused Cookie to perk up, but he quickly drifted back to sleep.

Robin's anxiety turned to fear. She questioned her sanity. It was impossible to make sense of what had just happened, especially after the earlier events. Trying to analyze it felt pointless. She got out of bed and went downstairs. Matt would be home soon, and the thought gave her something to cling to.

The fatigue was overwhelming. Robin knew she wouldn't be able to function at work. She phoned the assistant director and reported that she was ill. Even attempting her job felt impossible. Her mind was too scattered.

As she walked into the kitchen to make a cup of hot chocolate, a sharp pain shot through her ankle. She grabbed it instinctively. Lifting the leg of her pajama pants, she found faint but unmistakable bruises. They were shaped like fingers.

A shudder ran down her spine, and nausea rose in her throat. She must be losing her mind. She wanted to tell Matt, but she feared he would question her stability.

Cookie sat patiently by the west entrance. Robin opened the door and watched him scurry outside. When she returned to the stove, waiting for the milk to warm, heavy footsteps echoed in the upstairs hallway.

Her stomach dropped. She closed her eyes as terror settled over her. She pressed her palms to her face, desperate to block out the sound. She wanted to scream.

Coming back to herself, she walked into the parlor and grabbed her phone from her purse. Her fingers trembled as she texted Matt, begging him to come home. She couldn't stand another moment in the house alone. The night had become too much to process.

A moment later, his reply came: *What's wrong? Everything okay?*

She typed furiously: No! Everything is not okay! Just get home!

The ringing landline startled her. She rushed to the wall phone and answered without greeting him.

"What's wrong?" Matt asked.

Her voice trembled as she tried to stay composed. "I don't know if I'm okay, Matt. I feel like I'm going crazy."

"Robin, this isn't like you," he said gently. "You're calm and grounded. Are you hurt?"

"You have to come home. I don't know if I can do this anymore," she said through clenched teeth.

"Okay. Okay," he replied, steadying his voice. "I'll wrap some things up and be home in about twenty minutes."

"I need you here now."

"Honey, I'll get there as fast as I can. Okay?"

"Just get here," she said sharply, hanging up before he could answer.

She opened the kitchen door to let Cookie back in. She no longer cared about the hot chocolate. She just wanted her life to feel normal again. She wanted confirmation that she wasn't losing her mind.

She walked to the couch, pulled her knees to her chest, and wrapped her arms tightly around them. Tears overwhelmed her, and she sobbed helplessly. Cookie hopped onto the couch and nudged himself beside her, resting his head against her ribs.

The sound of a truck engine outside signaled Matt's arrival. She heard it shut off, and moments later the kitchen door opened and closed. She couldn't bring herself to move.

After he set his keys in the basket on the wall, he walked into the living room and sat beside her. He placed the back of his hand to her forehead. She wasn't warm.

"Baby, tell me what's happening," Matt said.

Slowly, she met his gaze. "I think I'm losing my mind, Matt."

"Why do you think you're going crazy?" he asked gently.

Without speaking, Robin pulled up the leg of her pajama pants and revealed the bruises on her ankle.

"What did you do?"

"I didn't do this," she said, her voice hollow. Her gaze was lifeless, something unfamiliar even to Matt.

"Who did this to you?" He leaned closer. "These look like finger marks, Robin. Who did this?"

"Not who, Matt. What."

He froze, words failing him.

"I can't sleep anymore," she continued. "Tonight something was in this house. The doors slammed upstairs. I heard footsteps. It was so loud I thought someone was going to come through the ceiling. Cookie acted like he was going to tear something apart—and he pissed himself."

She wiped her tears and kept going, her voice unsteady. "Something touched me. Someone spoke to me."

"Spoke to you?" His discomfort showed in his expression.

"The voice asked me for help. I was overwhelmed by sadness and grief. It felt like someone had died. Then there was giggling, and a flash of light. I know I sound insane, but I don't know how much more I can take. I tried to sleep, and something yanked me out of bed by my ankle." Fresh tears spilled over. "Am I going crazy? Schizophrenic? Having a breakdown?"

Matt pulled her close as she wept. She shook violently with emotion.

"Honey, you're sleep deprived. Do you know what that can do to a person? What you're describing could all be exhaustion. You are one of the sanest people I know."

"How do you explain the bruises?" she whispered.

"Maybe you hit the wooden bedpost in your sleep."

"You said it yourself. These are fingerprints," she insisted, pulling away to point at them.

"What can I do? Tell me how to help."

"Is there any way you can work days? I know it's a huge ask. You told me once you'd switch if it meant keeping us healthy. I'm scared, Matt. I feel like buying this house was a mistake. I love it, but being here without you terrifies me. Things are happening. I'll leave if I have to. I'll stay in a hotel."

He stroked her hair, trying desperately to calm her. "It's going to be alright. I promise. We'll figure it out."

"I don't think you heard me," she said quietly. "I am not spending another night alone in this house."

"Listen," he said softly, meeting her eyes. "Why don't you spend the day at Wendy's?"

She shook her head before he could finish. "No. I want you here. I need you, Matt."

"Okay." He stood and headed toward the basement.

Robin lay down on the couch and pulled the warm blanket over her. The morning sun filtered through the windows, and she couldn't believe how relieved she was just to see daylight. The exhaustion was unlike anything she had ever felt, settling deeper with each passing day.

She drifted off as faint voices hummed from the basement. Cookie soon jumped onto the couch and curled up on her feet, his favorite place despite the plush dog bed upstairs.

The soft clatter of dishes came from the kitchen, followed by the beep of the microwave. Robin slipped into a deeper sleep.

Hours later, she opened her eyes. She took stock of her body and mind. It was the best sleep she had had in months. Turning onto her back, she stretched. Cookie was gone. The living room was peaceful, nothing like the suffocating tension that had consumed the night before.

Sitting up, she rubbed her eyes and decided to eat. She made a peanut butter sandwich and poured a glass of milk, then retreated to the parlor to check emails and catch up on some work.

Footsteps sounded above her. Her body tensed, but then Matt descended the stairs quickly. Relief washed over her.

"It's taken care of," he said, appearing in the doorway. "I'll start days next week. I took a couple of sick days too."

Robin nodded gratefully. "I appreciate it, Matt."

He returned to the living room and stared out the west windows. The mid-morning fog still clung to the field. A woman walked toward the O'Bryans' house. She wasn't Mrs. O'Bryan. This woman was younger, dressed in a long white gown with puffy sleeves, glowing faintly. Her figure was nearly transparent.

Matt rubbed his eyes hard. When he opened them again, the figure was gone. He shook his head, blaming exhaustion, and walked upstairs to lie down.

24

A woman screamed as she ran down a dark hallway. The sound echoed in a way that felt stretched and warped. Robin could not tell where the walls began or ended. She stumbled into a room that seemed to pull her toward it. Bodies were piled up on the floor. Young women. Still. Silent. Their skin looked drained of color, as if the room had taken it from them. Blood streaked the walls in uneven trails.

In the center of the room, a pregnant woman lay on a wooden table. Her long black hair hung over the edges like heavy strands of rope. Her eyes darted from side to side, wild with fear, but the two men beside her remained motionless. Their faces were blank. Only their eyes were alive with something Robin did not recognize as human.

Robin stood in the corner. She did not remember walking there. She tried to step forward, but her legs felt fixed to the floor. Her fingers curled into fists as a cold pressure built in her chest.

The woman on the table turned her head toward Robin. The movement was slow and thick, like it crossed through water. "Help me," she cried. Robin tried again to move, but her feet would not respond. "They are going to kill me," the woman pleaded. "Please. They are going to take my baby." Her body strained helplessly against the bindings.

The men lifted their heads at the same time. Their slow, unnatural smiles crept upward. The taller man raised a knife. For a moment Robin could not tell if he was inches away or impossibly distant. Space shifted like a mirage.

He plunged the blade into the woman's abdomen. The scream that followed cracked through the air. Robin covered her ears, but the sound seemed to vibrate inside her skull.

"Stop," she cried. "Please. Stop." Her voice dissolved as the room blurred. A different sound pushed through the chaos. A familiar voice. Real.

"Robin. Honey, wake up."

She jolted upright in bed, breathing unsteadily. The dark of the bedroom felt different than the dark of the dream. This one stayed still. Matt sat beside her, startled awake. "Robin, are you okay? You were having a nightmare."

She blinked, trying to separate what she saw from where she was. The images clung to her. They did not fade the way normal dreams did. "Ye... yes," she whispered. She gave a shaky nod. "I am alright."

"You want to tell me about it."

"No," she said. "I just want to forget it." But she knew she would not. The scene was too clear. Too specific. Her hands trembled as she tried to unclench them. "I am sorry I woke you."

"It is okay," he said as they settled back into the bed. He wrapped his arm around her, and she rested her head against his chest. His heartbeat was steady. Real. Grounding. "You sure you are alright"

"I think so," she said, though her voice held uncertainty. The nightmare still pressed at the edges of her awareness. The images had weight. They felt like memory rather than imagination. She felt a familiar hum beneath her skin. It was the same sensation she felt during readings, during visions, during moments she could not explain to anyone but herself.

Sleep tugged at her again, but the unease did not leave. Her final words were barely audible. "Something about that was not mine," she whispered. "Something is trying to get through."

She drifted off with her heart still racing, aware that the darkness waiting for her was watching.

25

As time went by, Robin tried to push the paranormal experiences down into her core. Despite her efforts, nevertheless, she was haunted by the disturbing dream. Her entire life's mission had been to help people, and the image of the woman lying helplessly on the wooden table reminded her just how helpless she truly was. At times she felt intense guilt. She wondered if the dream might be a message with a much deeper meaning. Perhaps it was meant to guide her in some way. Still the feelings of hopelessness worsened and her battle with depression truly began.

In January, before the major incidents in the house escalated, Olivia had turned seven. Now it was May, and Robin turned twenty-seven. The warmer weather allowed Robin to begin planting flowers around the property. The yardwork seemed to be continuous. Due to the size of the property, it took an entire day to mow. Matt often spent his entire Sunday with that task as Robin worked in all of the flowerbeds with the landscaping projects.

As Robin enjoyed some time on the porch swing, she remembered fondly that a year ago, she'd met Matt. She couldn't believe it had already been a year. Time seemed to pass so quickly at times. Yet at other times, it dragged on.

Closing her eyes, she let the gentle wind brush against her skin. She heard the screen door close and opened her eyes. Matt stood beside her. He looked down at her as she glanced up at him. "Everyone will be here soon," he said

"I know. I need to get dressed," she replied as she stood up

When she opened the door, she saw a large glass vase filled with roses sitting on the kitchen island. Her cheeks flushed pink and her heart skipped with excitement. She walked to the flowers, sniffed them, and noticed an envelope dangling off of one of the stems. Handwritten on the front was her name. She took the card from the envelope and read the message silently:

My lover, this month represents one year of knowing you and your birthday. I count myself lucky to be the man you've chosen to spend the rest of your life with. I love you very much.

Robin's eyes filled with joyful tears. She felt Matt's arms wrap around her. "They are absolutely beautiful," she said, her voice shaking with emotion.

"They pale in comparison to you."

She turned to him with a smirk. "That was quite a line," she said through laughter.

"I'm waxing poetic here," he said with a grin.

"I got you something, too," she admitted.

Matt scowled. "It's your birthday, not mine," he argued.

"But it is our one-year anniversary in a way," She broke the embrace and held out her hand. "Come with me."

They ascended the stairs and walked into the master bedroom. On the bed lay a large rectangular box. Matt walked to it and they sat on the bed. He took the box into his lap as Robin stood in the doorway watching. Lifting the lid, he put it aside and pushed the tissue paper aside. He furrowed his eyebrows. "I'm confused," he said as he peered into the box.

Robin pursed her lips and walked in. She sat beside him. "It's for our trip that we shouldn't go on," she laughed.

He glanced at her and then looked back into the box. His laughter carried through the room as he pulled out a pair of tropical printed swimming trunks and a pair of sunglasses. He shook his head in amusement.

"You gave me a straw hat. So, I thought trunks and sunglasses may be useful."

"You didn't think it was a good idea for us to go on a trip," he reminded her.

"I know. Maybe someday though?" she said as she playfully pushed against his shoulder.

He leaned over and kissed her lips. "I love it," he whispered.

The light kiss turned into one much more passionate After a brief love-making session, they lay on the bed, their clothing strung all over the floor of the room. "We have guests coming," Robin said softly as she ran her fingers through his dark hair.

"I suppose we should get up and get dressed, huh?" he asked with his eyes closed.

Robin simply nodded.

After putting their clothing back on and cleaning up the bed, they went to work preparing for the day's plans. Bill, Leah, Terri, and Wendy arrived for dinner. They sat around the dining room table laughing and talking without a worry in the world. Finally, things felt normal to Robin for just a moment. The sadness lifted as she enjoyed the company and companionship of her friends.

After dinner, Matt and Bill sat on the west porch at the checkerboard table. Leah and Wendy relaxed in the rocking chairs. Terri sat on the porch steps with his back against one of the wooden pillars. He watched the game between Matt and Bill. Robin relaxed in the swing with Cookie laying right next to her.

A door slammed inside and they heard something crash to the floor. Cookie immediately perked up. Robin's eyes flashed with fear. Matt stood and nodded. "I got it," he said calmly as he made eye contact with Robin.

The others sat still, all of them wearing expressions of confusion. "Sometimes the breeze can catch the doors," Matt explained to the others.

He calmly opened the screen door and walked into the living room. As he neared the basement door, he saw a shattered picture frame on the floor. He knelt down and began cleaning up the glass. He sighed as he realized which photograph had been affected. It was their first Christmas picture. They were standing by the tree together smiling as if they hadn't a care in the world. As he recalled, it was a happy time.

When he finished, Matt walked back out to rejoin the others. They all looked at him expectantly. "Wind," he said shortly.

Robin didn't buy it. Their eyes met. Dred and anxiety made it hard for her to breathe. "What fell?" she asked.

"It was just a picture," he said nonchalantly. "Frame is broken but the print isn't hurt."

Without further incident, the evening continued on. Once everyone left, Robin began cleaning up the dishes. She stood at the sink rinsing them off trying hard to put the shattering picture frame out of her thoughts.

She heard the stereo come on. An Elvis song played. Then she heard Matt singing along. She couldn't help but smile. She knew him all too well. He was trying to lighten the mood and perhaps get lucky again. She smirked as she put another plate into the dishwasher.

Matt's voice echoed as he entered the kitchen. "Shall I stay? Would it be a sin?"

Robin turned her head and looked over her shoulder at him as he continued serenading her, his arms outstretched as if he were performing on stage. She chuckled lightly.

"Dance with me," he said as he walked closer to her.

"Now?" she asked as she put a glass in the dishwasher.

"You have no excuse not to. I'm the best dance teacher there is, remember?" he boasted.

"I remember," she said as she grabbed the dry dishtowel.

Matt was behind her and turned her around slowly. He took the dishtowel from her and tossed it onto the counter. Taking her by the hand, he led her to the middle of the kitchen. They swayed as the music played. Robin rested her head on Matt's chest, his chin against her forehead. He softly sung to her as Robin laced her fingers through his belt loops.

"We need to start going out more," he whispered. "I miss dancing with you."

"Why go out when we can dance right here?" she asked quietly.

"I guess you're right. I just miss dates, you know?"

"Marriage changes things. Time changes everything," she replied.

"I don't want us to change. I want us to age like fine wine... only get better with age," Matt said with sincerity.

After their dance, Robin went back to the dishes and Matt went upstairs to shower. When he was finished, he walked into the master bedroom to find Robin sitting in bed reading. He stood in the doorway gazing at her sensually. He watched as she turned the page, her glasses sitting perfectly on her nose.

He became aroused as he admired her. Her shiny, dark hair hung in curls on her shoulders. Her flawless skin against the sheer material of her night gown made him yearn to touch her. So, he walked to the bed and sat down in front of her.

"What are you reading?" he asked.

"It's a book on paranormal phenomenon."

"Whoa. No wonder you are having nightmares. You're scaring yourself to death."

She didn't reply. Finally, she made eye contact. She put her glasses on the nightstand and closed the book. An unspoken tension lingered between them as the sensual nature of the situation became evident. Matt leaned in close to her and, without taking his eyes away, he reached over to turn the light off.

Robin stood and pulled the night gown over her head. Matt helped her out of her panties. He then stood and took the towel from around his waist. He tossed it aside. Robin lay on the mattress awaiting his touch. He obliged, kissing her belly and touching her tenderly. Finding her inner thighs, he gently touched his lips to them. Robin twister her fingers into his hair as he licked her. "You always taste so good. Should I stop?" he asked as he teased her.

She grinned, "I didn't say you had to stop."

He teased her some more.

"Just come here," she demanded. She reached for him as he spread her legs apart. He pushed into her slowly as she wrapped her legs around his waist.

After a few strokes, they flipped over, Robin on top of him and Matt's back against the headboard. She moved slowly and deliberately, her hands resting on his shoulders, her mouth slightly opened. She moaned softly.

"Let go baby. Let me have all of you," he said softly as their eyes locked. He felt her tighten around him and the moans became louder as she closed her eyes and threw her head back. He leaned forward, pulled her hair away, and kissed her neck and shoulders.

Something across the room caught his eye. There was a man dressed in a turn-of-the-century tuxedo. Alarmed, he reared back and blinked his eyes several times. Finally, the apparition disappeared, but not before smiling at him and winking.

"What's wrong?" Robin asked. She stopped and assessed his expression. He was pale.

He pushed her off of him and stood up. Swiftly, he walked to the dresser and grabbed a pair of shorts.

"What is going on?" she insisted as she grabbed the gown off of the floor and dressed.

He still didn't answer her and instead walked to the doorway and looked into the hall. He shook his head as he tried to understand what he saw. He walked back to the bed and sat down.

"Matthew, what is wrong?" Robin asked again.

"It's nothing," he lied.

"It was obviously something," she argued. "You have never done that. Did I do something wrong?"

He turned to her and took her hands. "Oh no. No. Of course not. You did nothing wrong, Robin."

"Tell me what you saw, Matt," she insisted.

He stood and walked to his side of the bed. He sat down and leaned against the headboard again. "I could have sworn I saw a man standing in the doorway."

Robin shook her head in disgust. "There's something wrong with this house," she stated softly.

"I think I'm just tired," he replied as he pinched the bridge of his nose. "I saw a woman walking in the field, too. She was going toward the O'Bryan's place." He sighed and shrugged as he looked over at Robin. "And today I didn't leave the basement door open when we all went outside. It was shut. There's no way the wind could have caught it."

"Tell me what the woman in the field looked like," she insisted.

He described her.

"My nightmare," she murmured. She shared the dream with Matt.

His expression was that of pure astonishment. "So, do you think the woman in the field and the woman in your dream are the same person? That all of these things are related to one another somehow?"

"I think it's very possible," Robin answered. "I'm calling my dad. I'm going to ask him to bless the house. Maybe that will help."

"You don't believe in religion," Matt retorted.

She glared at him. "You may not believe in anything," she began. "But I can assure you, there is a world outside of our own. I've known it since I was a small child. This isn't the first time things like this have happened to me. I just wanted to believe these things wouldn't happen to me again."

Matt shook his head. "What do you mean?"

With a deep breath, Robin shared her childhood experiences. She explained that as a young girl she had seen and heard things that others couldn't. As she aged, she had become more open to things. She told Matt that she felt like her religious upbringing had blinded her in many ways, but the things that had happened to her were beyond explanation, especially the dreams and nightmares.

She told Matt that it had all begun at the age of four. An entity had made contact with her. It had been an old woman in her closet. Robin explained that she had told her brother, and that he had believed her, but when she confided in her mother and stepfather, they attributed it to a child's wild imagination.

Robin went on to say that she had seen terrible things in the nightmares. Prayer had been the only way that she could settle her mind. She had been able to see things that she had no knowledge of... hangings, burnings, and other horrific deaths. She told Matt that she had come to believe that she was able to see into the past through her dreams.

"So, these are higher-level abilities? Like a sixth sense?" Matt asked.

"I think that I have a higher level of intuition which is why these things happen to me. I can feel residual energy."

"What's that?"

"Well, if something has happened here in this house, or in any space, sometimes I can pick up on the energy that's been left behind. If someone was hurt in this house or died here, it's likely that I'm picking up on that. I haven't had things like this happen to me since

I was in middle school. I shut all of this down. It was just too much to try to carry when I was younger," Robin expressed.

"I'm still having a difficult time understanding this, Robin. I've never been in a situation that I just couldn't explain. Everything can be explained," he rationalized.

"Yes, it can be explained. The explanations, however, may be rooted in the past though or rooted in things you can't see anymore."

"I don't know," he said reluctantly. "It does sound like the overactive imagination of a child. You are very creative and highly intelligent. It's not unusual for children who are intellectually gifted to think outside of the box. You can probably access parts of your brain that others can't."

Robin shook her head. She was obviously disheartened. "I'm going to sleep. There's no point in talking about this any further." She turned over, flipped out the light, and pulled the covers up over her shoulders. She left Matt to sort through his thoughts.

26

Sunday afternoon offered a chance to get some fresh air. Just as he did every Sunday, Matt mowed the property. He needed space, not only from the house but from Robin. The experience of the previous night had left him shaken in a way he refused to acknowledge. He wanted to pretend nothing had happened, to bury it under routine and noise.

Robin spent the afternoon in the basement folding laundry. The more she replayed things, the more convinced she became that a blessing might help. Her stepdad had never agreed with her change of faith, yet he respected it. He had always encouraged her to seek her own truth, even when he did not understand her path.

She crossed the basement and lifted the cordless phone from its cradle. After dialing Richard's number, she waited through several rings before his melodic hello came through.

"Hey Daddy," she replied, her voice weighted with fatigue.

"What's going on, ladybug? Something's wrong."

"Daddy," she began carefully, "I wondered if you'd be willing to do a blessing on the house."

"Why don't you tell me what's been happening, Baby Girl? You don't sound like yourself."

"I just think a blessing should be performed. It's good practice, right?" she said, trying to sound casual even as her throat tightened.

"We'll be there."

Outside, the mower hummed across the yard. The steady whirl of the blades usually calmed Matt, but today his nerves sat too close to the surface. When he noticed Mr. O'Bryan waving from the property line, he slowed the mower and cut the engine. He hopped off, forced a smile, and met him halfway.

Curtis O'Bryan had been one of the first to welcome Matt and Robin when they moved in. He had seemed genuinely relieved to have neighbors again, especially a young couple willing to take on the old house.

He and Katie brought dishes, desserts, and easy conversation. They had spent several evenings together at the O'Bryans, swapping stories and slowly building a friendship.

"So y'all made it through the winter, I see," Curtis said with a grin.

"It'll be June before long," Matt replied as he took off his ball cap. He wiped his sweaty brow with his sleeve, squinting against the sun before putting the hat back on.

"You and the wife doing okay?" Curtis asked.

"She's tired, but we both are. Seems like all we do is work." Matt tried to keep his tone light, but his eyes betrayed the strain.

"I remember those days. Katie was a schoolteacher. Felt like we never saw each other much before we retired. Don't know how we raised three kids. You two expecting any little ones yet?"

"Not yet," Matt answered politely.

Curtis nodded toward the house. "I see a little girl playing over there."

"She's mine from a previous marriage. I promised I'd bring her to meet your grandkids."

"You should. We'll have our granddaughters most of the summer. They'd love a new friend."

"I'll send Olivia over. She's staying the week." Matt paused, tension creeping back into his shoulders. "Let me ask you something, Curt."

Curtis crossed his arms. "Go on."

"The people who lived here before. Did they ever say anything about strange things happening in the house?"

Curtis pursed his lips as he considered the question. "Well, the house sat empty for about twelve years before y'all bought it. The folks who lived here before kept to themselves. They'd say hello every now and then, but they were pretty introverted. They never told us anything strange." He studied Matt's face. "Everything okay?"

"Oh, yeah. Just curious." Matt tried to shrug it off, but he was terrible at hiding emotion.

"You sure you two are alright?" Curtis asked gently.

"Oh, it's nothing serious, but Robin and I hear things sometimes. We see things every now and then."

Curtis glanced toward the house. "That place has a long history. If you want my advice, do some research. Might help explain a few things."

Matt nodded. "Makes sense. Well, I better get back to it. I'll send Olivia over when she gets here."

Curtis headed home, leaving Matt more unsettled than before.

An hour later, Sheryl's car pulled into the lane. Robin was already outside waiting, arms open. Olivia bolted from the car and into her embrace. Sheryl waved as she backed down the drive.

Matt returned to mowing, but his gaze drifted toward the house again and again. When something moved in the study window, he froze. A figure stood there, motionless. He squinted, trying to tell if it was male or female. Then the figure turned its head and stared directly at him.

Matt jumped off the mower and sprinted toward the house. He threw open the screen door and took the stairs two at a time. Robin followed behind him, startled by the urgency in his footsteps.

He burst into the study, ready to fight, ready to catch whoever had invaded their home. But the room was empty. The emptiness only fueled his fury.

"What the hell is going on here!" he shouted.

"Matt, what's wrong?" Robin asked as she rushed in.

Olivia peeked inside. Robin immediately redirected her. "Go play in the basement for a minute, honey. I'll be down soon."

Matt collapsed into the rolling chair, defeated. Robin crossed her arms and waited, silently urging him to speak.

"Okay, Robin," he said finally, "I think you might be right. Something is going on in this house."

She knelt in front of him. "What happened?"

"I talked to Curt for a bit and then looked up here. Someone was standing in this room, looking right at me. I saw the bowtie. The tuxedo. It was the same thing I saw in our doorway last night."

Robin cupped his cheek. "My dad is coming to bless the house. Everything will get better."

"There has to be an explanation," Matt insisted. His neck vein bulged with tension. Logic had always been his anchor, but now it was slipping.

Robin offered the only comfort she could. "We'll figure it out together."

By late afternoon, she returned to the laundry. Music played quietly on her phone until it abruptly faded and stopped. The battery was full, yet the phone refused to play. Before she could curse it again, the air shifted.

Cold slid across her skin like a sheet of ice. Goose pimples rose instantly. Her breath puffed visibly in front of her.

Then something invisible wrapped around her neck.

She clawed at her throat, desperate for air. Her feet felt as if they were leaving the ground. Tears blurred her vision as she fought against the tightening force. She could not speak. She could not scream. Panic pulsed through her chest in frantic waves.

The pressure released suddenly. She collapsed onto the table, gasping. Once her voice returned, she screamed for Matt.

He raced down the stairs, panic spilling from his face.

"Robin!"

She shook her head, barely able to form words. "I was being hanged."

"Hung?" he corrected, confused.

She explained everything, then fell into his chest, sobbing. He held her tightly, whispering reassurance even as fear gnawed at him.

Afterward, she escaped to the master bedroom. She needed grounding. She unrolled her yoga mat, sat cross-legged, and practiced her breathing. The rhythm settled her, though her hands still trembled.

Fifteen minutes later, Matt stood in the doorway watching her.

"What were you doing?" he asked.

"Meditating."

"Do you do that a lot?"

"Off and on. It's good for trauma. It forces the brain and body to calm down. Anyone can benefit from it."

"Do you pray, too?" he asked softly, genuinely.

"Sometimes. Gratitude practice. Thanking my Creator. Sometimes I commune with my spirit guides."

"And after what happened downstairs, you're calm enough to do this?"

"No. I made myself. Mindfulness helps regulate the nervous system. Even when I'm a mess, I trust it will eventually help."

He shook his head. "I don't understand any of this."

"I have books if you want to read them," she offered.

"I think I'll pass," he admitted. "But if it helps you and makes you happy, keep doing it."

The phone rang. Robin hurried downstairs.

"Ladybug," Richard said, "we can't make it today. Your mama came down with something. Maybe next weekend."

Robin's heart sank. "Yes. That's fine."

She hung up and told Matt. His disappointment mirrored her own.

That night, sleep came reluctantly. Matt drifted in and out until he heard a voice. Olivia's. She was talking to someone.

He checked the clock. A little after four.

He walked quietly to her room. Through the door he heard her carrying on a full conversation, though only her voice was audible.

He eased the door open. Her nightlight cast a soft glow across the room. She sat upright on her bed.

"Hey Princess," he said gently. "Can't sleep?"

"I was talking to my friend," she said. "She wakes me up sometimes."

"What friend?"

"She's a little girl. She told me her mommy and daddy don't live here anymore."

Matt tried to smile. "An imaginary friend? What's she look like?"

"She's older than me. Long curly black hair. A red ribbon. She's nice, but she gets scared."

He nodded, humoring her.

"She said she loves it when you and Robin dance in the kitchen."

Matt froze. Olivia had never seen them dance. Not once.

"She says she misses her mommy, but Robin makes her feel safe. Cookie plays with her, too."

Matt swallowed hard. His mouth went dry. "Olly, is she in here right now?"

"No. She left when she heard you get up. You scared her."

"What's her name?"

"Emma. She lives in the woods out back. She told me the man in the house is mean. He hurts her. She said a lady asked Robin for help. The bad man hurt the lady and her baby. She said there's something else in the house that is very scary."

Matt felt the blood drain from his face. He told Olivia to get some rest, then went downstairs in a daze.

He leaned on the counter, staring into the dark yard. His hands trembled. For the first time in his life, he felt a fear that cut through logic and training.

Then arms slipped around his waist.

He exhaled and reached down to touch her hands. But he felt only fabric. No skin.

He spun and pressed himself against the counter. "Who are you?" he whispered. "What do you want from us?"

No response. Only silence.

Footsteps approached. Robin walked into the kitchen, rubbing her eyes.

"Matt, what's wrong?" she asked, wrapping her arms around him. "You're shaking. Baby, what is it? Are you sick?"

"It touched me," he said, voice broken.

"What touched you?"

He explained everything, including Olivia's conversation with Emma.

Robin covered her mouth in shock.

"I felt arms around me," he whispered. "I thought it was you. But there was nothing."

"Oh God, Matt," she said as she held him.

The moment steadied until she suddenly flinched.

"Honey, stop it."

"Stop what?"

"Stop pulling my hair."

"I'm not pulling your hair. My hands are right here."

Her breath caught. "Something just pulled my hair."

Matt pulled her close again as her tears gathered.

"I don't know," he said. "I don't know what's happening."

27

Robin stood at the top of the stairs looking down into the hallway. A large red ball bounced down the stairs. She ran after it, but then fell. The sensation of falling woke her up.

She sat up in bed and tried to catch her breath. Matt was beside her sleeping peacefully. Taking account of her surroundings, nothing seemed strange. The sunlight through the heavy wooden shades began to light up the room. Cookie slept on his bed. The white noise coming from the box fan on the floor helped her calm down.

The dreams meant something. It was a mystery though. Robin still didn't understand what was going on. She wanted to, nonetheless. Thankfully, her stepfather and her mother would be arriving soon. Then maybe there would be peace in the house.

After preparing for the day, Robin busied herself making a meat and vegetable tray. She prepared the east porch with an array of condiments and drinks. Her folks hadn't visited them since they'd moved in. She wanted to make a good impression.

As they sat outside enjoying the light lunch, they conversed about insignificant things like the weather. Still, Robin knew that her cool exterior was something Richard could easily see through. And he did.

"You guys doing okay?" he asked with concern in his tone.

She nodded. "We're okay."

He shook his head, "Little girl, you can't lie to me. You wouldn't have asked me to do a blessing if everything was fine." He pulled the napkin from his lap and put it on the table and continued.

"I'm your daddy. I can always tell when you're not telling the truth. Ever since you were small, you get a look on your face that lets me know you want to say more, but you either don't know how or you don't want to tell me what's really going on."

She dropped her head and rested her hands on the tabletop. Then she felt Matt's hand on top of hers. She listened as her husband took the lead. He explained the strange incidents in the home. He tried to provide as much detail as he could. He concluded by saying, "I'm not sure what to believe anymore or what to believe in."

"Son," Richard began, "there's a fine line between what we can see and what we can't. What's real in this world and what's real in the next one. It says in the Bible that we don't fight against flesh and blood, but against principalities and things unseen."

Matt shook his head. "You'll have to forgive me, but I don't know much about the Bible. What does that mean?"

"It means that each day we struggle against the spiritual world, which is a world we just can't see. Things that we think are just coincidence or luck, well they aren't. Sounds to me like that's what you've been doing. It explains why you both look so tired."

"I don't know what is going on," Matt continued. "I know that at times both of us feel like we've lost our minds. And I'm not a religious man so I'm at a complete loss with this stuff."

"Well, looks like we're all finished with lunch," Richard said. "Let's get started with the blessing." He stood and walked inside as the others followed. He grabbed his bag off the couch and took out his Bible.

As he and Amy walked from room to room reciting scripture. Robin and Matt observed. Robin understood what she was seeing. Matt was at a loss. He had only met Richard once. He was a humble, back-woodsy, easy-going man. While Richard blessed the house, he spoke with authority. He dabbed olive oil on each of the thresholds in the house as he rebuked any unwelcomed spirits and blessed each room with the light of God.

Something changed when Richard reached the threshold to the study. He dabbed the olive oil on his finger and reached up above his head. His expression contorted as he spoke. "Honey, it's freezing in this room."

Matt quickly interjected. "This is the coldest room in the house. It always has been."

"There's a reason for that," Amy said without offering to expound. Still, the blessing didn't cause a flurry of activity. So, they moved on to the yard. While Robin and Matt stood on the east porch, they watched as Richard and Amy moved about the property.

Amy and Richard came back to the porch. "This place has a history," Richard said.

"What do you mean?" Matt asked.

"Think of the people who have lived and died here, let alone on the land during its tribal times," Richard answered.

Amy spoke. "If you two truly want to know what's happening here, investigate your house's history. I think you may find some answers there."

28

An important career opportunity arose for Matt at the hospital. The Chief of Medicine had retired, and the board of directors was anxious to fill the vacancy. Interviews had been underway for months, yet none of the applicants had impressed them. Matt had wrestled with the decision for weeks. He talked it through with Robin late at night when the house felt calm enough for honesty. Eventually, he applied. He was the youngest candidate, but the promotion came with a substantial pay raise and the possibility of paying off Pikeview Manor earlier than planned. The idea of stability comforted them both more than either admitted aloud, especially after the chaos of the spring.

Finally, after more than a year of waiting, the house, now officially recognized as Pikeview Manor, was placed on the registry. The extra funding eased some of the financial strain and made the future feel more manageable. It also brought a strange mix of pride and unease. Sometimes the house felt like a prize, and sometimes it felt like something that had chosen them rather than the other way around.

Robin opened the east porch door and stepped into the family room. She heard Matt's voice coming from the kitchen, low and animated. He was clearly on the phone. She grabbed a bottle of water from the fridge and twisted off the cap, listening to the lightness in his tone. It had been a long time since she had heard that kind of excitement in him.

When he finished, he turned toward her with a smile that brightened his whole face. "I got the job," he said, breathless with disbelief and joy.

Robin clapped and bounced on her toes before hurrying to him. She wrapped her arms around him. "That is great! I'm so proud of you!"

Matt lifted her off the ground and spun her in a tight circle. For a moment, everything felt simple again, as if the house were just a house and their life had always been this uncomplicated. He set her back down and kissed her deeply. One kiss led to another, and they soon found their way upstairs.

After a long, intimate celebration, they settled into each other's arms. The room felt calm and warm, but beneath that peace was a fragile undercurrent neither acknowledged. Moments like this felt precious, almost delicate, as if joy needed to be held carefully.

Matt kissed her forehead and traced slow lines across her back. Robin rested against him, quiet and distant. Her thoughts drifted somewhere he could not see. "What are you thinking about?" he asked softly.

She lifted her head, then rolled onto her side to face him. "Can I ask you something?"

"Anything."

"Do you want kids?"

He shifted onto his elbow and searched her expression. "Of course I do. I just didn't know if you wanted to start trying. We never really talked about it, not seriously. And I also wanted us to feel better about living here."

Robin hesitated. "I am still sort of unsure about the house." It wasn't fear exactly, but there were moments when she felt it watching, weighing, waiting.

"I get that," he said quietly. "When it comes to kids, though, I'm ready when you are. I just wasn't sure if you wanted some time for us. After everything that's happened, I figured we both needed room to breathe."

"I'm torn about it, to be honest."

"I understand." His smile softened. "I like having you all to myself, but I would also love to have a little version of you and me running around, too."

She smiled back at him, though uncertainty flickered in her eyes. The idea warmed her and frightened her at the same time.

"Listen," he said gently as he leaned in and kissed her shoulder, "you tell me when you're ready, and we'll go for it. Okay?"

29

The peace they had found in late summer carried them into fall, but as the holidays approached, life began shifting in quieter, heavier ways.

December came in like a lion with a major snowstorm. Matt's new responsibilities at the hospital consumed him, making things around the house feel even chillier. Robin understood, though. He was working diligently to prove he deserved the job. Still, the extra money and the weight of his new role did nothing to ease the loneliness she felt once again.

To compensate, Robin changed her work schedule to match Matt's. She worked four ten-hour days with Friday, Saturday, and Sunday off. Her days began at 7:30 a.m. and ended at 6 p.m. Cookie was dropped off at doggy daycare by 7:00 a.m. and picked up by 6:15 p.m.

It was well after dark as Robin strolled back up the lane after checking the mailbox. As she neared the house, she paused to admire the structure and the scenery. The Christmas tree in the parlor cast a soft glow across the snow beneath the window. Cookie ran ahead of her, frolicking through the drifts.

As she drew closer, something in her periphery caught her attention. A woman stood in the east field. Robin took in the woman's appearance. She wore a thin white nightgown, far too light for the freezing temperatures. It didn't make sense.

Robin started toward her, prepared to assist. "Miss, can I help you?" she called out. The woman turned and looked over her shoulder. Her eyes were hollow, and a deep sadness emanated from them.

"Miss," Robin continued as the woman began to walk away. "It's cold out here. Do you need help?"

A thunderous crash sounded behind her. Robin turned back toward the house. A planter lay shattered on the east porch, and Cookie hunkered down in shame. She shook her head, then looked back toward the field. The woman was gone.

Ignoring her instincts, Robin walked to the porch and bent down to gather the broken ceramic pieces. After cleaning up, she went into the house and tossed them into the trash. The loud ring of the landline startled her, and her heart skipped a beat. She answered. Matt's voice came through the receiver. "I'm so sorry, but I'm going to be late again."

"Again?"

"I'm really sorry, but there's just so much paperwork to catch up on. This job is nothing like I thought it would be," he admitted.

"Can't you bring it home?" she asked.

"I can't. I have to work on it here."

Robin's tolerance began to weaken. "Fine," she bit out.

"I'm sorry. I promise I'll make it up to you," he said.

"Okay." She capitulated, unsure she had another choice.

After a shower, Robin settled into bed with a book. Drowsiness overtook her, and she nestled under the warm covers. She drifted off, saddened by the empty space beside her.

A few hours later, Matt pulled into the garage. He got out of the truck and walked to the kitchen door. He pushed it open just as the grandfather clock chimed. It was 10:30 p.m. The glow from the electric candles illuminated the empty rooms. He flipped on the light and saw a note on the counter. He walked over and read it:

Dinner's in the oven.

A twinge of guilt shot through him. He knew he was leaving Robin alone too much.

As he opened the oven, he heard Cookie bounding down the stairs. The dog greeted him happily. Matt knelt to pet him, then retrieved the leftovers. He heated the meatloaf and potatoes and retired to the living room to watch a little television. He needed to decompress.

After eating, the television couldn't hold his attention. Exhaustion tugged at him. His eyes grew heavy. Then he heard Robin's sweet voice calling his name.

"Just a minute," he replied as he stood and walked through the kitchen and up the stairs.

He turned into their bedroom and saw a tall, dark figure standing on Robin's side of the bed. Instinct took over. He flipped on the light, ready to attack whoever had gotten into the house.

"Get away from her!" he shouted.

Robin shot up in bed. She rubbed her eyes and squinted. "Why are you shouting?" she asked, her voice raspy from sleep.

Disbelief paralyzed him, but he forced himself forward. He plopped onto the bed and shook his head.

"Matt," she said as she threw the covers off and moved to his side. She sat beside him and gently turned his face toward hers. "Matt, talk to me. What's wrong?"

He struggled to form the words but finally managed. "I thought you were calling for me. So I came upstairs. I saw a... I don't know what it was... it was standing beside you. Then when I turned the light on, it disappeared."

"I'm okay," she said gently, rubbing his back.

"What I saw reminded me of something from a horror film," he continued. "It scared the hell out of me. I thought someone had broken into the house, but what I saw was far too large to be a man." He stood and began pacing. "This isn't over, is it?" he said quietly. Rage welled inside him. "This isn't over!" he shouted. "The blessing didn't work, Robin!" The venom in his tone made her flinch. "Got any more suggestions?" he barked.

"I... I don't..." she stuttered.

"You don't what?" he yelled. "Robin, I can't wrap my head around this! I'm a very logical man. And this... this has no logic! I can't believe this is happening! These things don't happen in real life!"

"Matt, this isn't my fault," she said defensively. "Why are you screaming at me?" Tears stung her eyes.

"I didn't say it was your fault, damn it! I love this house," he insisted, still pacing. "And I love you. This house was an investment in us and it's turning into a ritualistic nightmare!"

Robin was speechless. She had never seen Matt react like this. His agitation triggered her. Her hands trembled, and her mind spiraled back into memories of Brett.

"Get out of my house!" he yelled as he shook his fist at the ceiling. "Just get out!"

Robin pushed through her fear and rushed to him. She placed her hands on his shoulders, tears streaming down her cheeks. "Shhh," she whispered as she wrapped him in her embrace. She felt him quivering against her.

"This is our house…" he whispered as he dropped to his knees and pressed his head against her breast.

30

Robin sat at her desk staring at the file that had made it onto the auditor's list. The State would be visiting soon to ensure the agency was compliant with mandates. Normally she would be hypervigilant about details, but the chaos at home made it nearly impossible to focus. Her exhaustion felt bone-deep. Her eyes even burned, as if she had cried more than she slept.

As he often did, Terri walked into her office without knocking. He paused when he saw her. "You okay? You look like you might be catching something."

Robin managed a thin smile. "I'm just tired."

He launched into a discussion about a case he was working on, but Robin's thoughts drifted. She couldn't stop thinking about Matt's panic, the anger that followed, or the fear in his eyes. She didn't blame him; she was terrified herself. Something about last night had shifted the ground beneath them.

Suddenly, she heard her name. "Robin, are you still there?" Terri waved a hand in front of her face.

She blinked and straightened. "Terri, I'm so sorry. What is it you need help with again?"

His expression softened from irritation to concern. "Are you okay? You and Matt doing alright?"

Robin exhaled. "If I told you what's really wrong, you wouldn't believe me."

"Try me."

She hesitated. As a clinician, saying the words out loud felt absurd, even reckless. But Terri wasn't just a coworker; he was Wendy's boyfriend, already woven into Robin's life, someone who had seen her under pressure before. And she was too overwhelmed to keep carrying this alone.

The hesitation cracked, and everything came out. She told him about the doors slamming, the apparitions, the dreams, the blessing that didn't seem to hold, and last night's encounter. She didn't realize until she spoke the words how much she had been keeping bottled up. For a moment, it felt like a weight lifted. Then reality settled again. Talking about it didn't solve anything.

"I think my house is haunted," she said quietly, surprised by how surreal it sounded.

Terri didn't laugh or dismiss her. "Believe it or not, I get it. My sister had trouble like that years ago. They had the home blessed and then cleansed. Big difference between the two. They finally got in touch with a paranormal investigation group."

Robin considered it. She had been avoiding researching the house, afraid of what she might uncover. "Maybe I need to start digging into Pikeview's history."

Terri nodded. "That might help. I'll see if my sister still has the number for that group."

Robin felt a small swell of relief. Not a solution, but a direction.

That evening, she picked Olivia up at Sheryl's for her holiday visit. The drive was quiet. Olivia had changed over the last few months, becoming withdrawn and guarded. Her grades were slipping. She wasn't participating in anything she used to enjoy, which immediately raised concern in Robin's professional instincts. She didn't press. Olivia needed safety, not pressure.

When they pulled into the garage, Robin was surprised to see Matt already home. The aroma of warm food met them as they stepped inside.

Olivia disappeared downstairs. Curious, Robin walked into the dining room and found candles lit and a place setting for two. Matt came down the stairs as she stepped into the kitchen.

"You're home early," she said, slipping out of her coat.

"I figured I'd surprise you." He pulled a glass dish from the oven. "Baked spaghetti. Told you I'd make it up to you."

His smile was genuine. Robin appreciated the effort, though a small part of her remained cautious. Emotional cracks didn't mend in one evening.

Later, after Olivia went upstairs to shower, Robin and Matt watched a movie. Something kept tugging at her.

"Are you okay?" Matt asked.

"Something's wrong with Olivia," she said quietly.

He frowned. "What do you mean? You think it's boys already?"

"No. She's too young for that. And this feels different."

"I'll talk to her."

Before he could stand, a bloodcurdling scream echoed from upstairs.

Both of them bolted up the stairs. Olivia stood in the bathroom wrapped in a towel, trembling so hard the droplets on the floor vibrated with her shaking.

Matt dropped to his knees. "Baby, what's wrong?"

She clung to him. "Daddy, don't let it hurt me."

"What? What hurt you?"

"I was drying off... the door was cracked... someone was staring at me. I saw something standing there. It wasn't Emma. It was something else." She swallowed hard. "Can I please sleep in your room tonight?"

"Sure," he said immediately. "Actually, let's sleep downstairs in front of the fire. All of us. Okay?"

She nodded.

Robin kept her voice steady. "Do you want me to braid your hair and help you get ready for bed?"

Another small nod.

While Robin helped her, the air felt heavy around them. Charged. Robin debated whether to ask but concern outweighed hesitation.

"Olly... is anything bothering you? Anything you want to talk about?"

"I'm fine," Olivia murmured.

Robin recognized the defensive wall. "You can talk to your dad or me about anything. We love you. What happened tonight was really scary. Is there anything else going on?"

"No," Olivia said quickly.

"It's okay to be afraid."

"I know. Just... don't leave me up here."

"I won't."

Once Olivia was settled downstairs watching a movie, she drifted into sleep.

A while later, Matt came up from the basement. Robin looked over. "Who were you talking to?"

"Your dad and my brother."

"Why?"

"Because I'm trying to understand what's happening in this house. I can't just ignore it anymore. You don't realize how hard this is for me."

Robin bristled gently. "I do, actually."

He exhaled. "Your dad thinks the blessing didn't work. He thinks this is something different."

Robin looked at Olivia's small, sleeping form. "He thinks it's demonic, doesn't he?"

Matt nodded. "Yes."

Robin nodded once, slowly. "I was raised in church. I know the signs. I think a lot of what's been going on here is human. But whatever you and Olivia are seeing is darker."

"I'm solution-oriented, Robin. What do we do? Move?"

"Terri told me about a paranormal investigation group. He's getting me the information."

"What is a paranormal investigation group?"

"People who can objectively assess hauntings. It's more legitimate than it sounds."

Matt rubbed his face. "I don't know what I believe anymore."

The next day, Terri handed her the number for the Midwest Ghost Hunters. She slipped it into her purse and exhaled.

Deep down, she hoped the dark activity would stop. She didn't mind the human spirits. But the others, the ones terrifying Matt and Olivia, those needed to be confronted.

And soon.

31

Weeks passed with no unusual activity in the house. The holidays came and went. The silence at Pikeview was a relief, but it also left more room for Robin to notice the distance growing between her and Matt. Continuing to work the four ten-hour shifts, she still had Fridays to herself. Today, she wanted to surprise Matt by taking him out to lunch. She had packed his favorite sandwiches in the old picnic basket, not to be cute, but because the familiarity of the gesture felt grounding. Their life had not felt normal in a long time, and she was trying to hold on to something solid.

She arrived at the hospital around 12:30 p.m. and walked into Matt's office suite, where she was greeted by his assistant.

Audrey Wheeler was very young and attractive. She had a beautifully symmetrical face with big blue eyes. Her full lips and high cheekbones accented her lovely features. Her long blonde hair hung in soft curls down her back. She typed diligently as she looked through thin wire-rimmed glasses perched on her nose.

Robin smiled as she approached. Matt had not mentioned hiring an assistant. The memory of his late nights at the hospital slipped into her thoughts, and insecurity began to mount.

"Can I help you?" Audrey asked.

"Is Matt here?" Robin replied with a pleasant smile.

"He is not seeing anyone right now," Audrey said, her tone polite but cool.

"I think he will see me," Robin said confidently.

"Is this urgent?"

Before Robin could respond, Matt's office door opened and he stepped out. He smiled when he saw her. "Hey there."

Robin returned the smile as he walked to her and kissed her forehead. "I brought you lunch," she said, lifting the basket slightly.

"Awesome. I'm starving." He turned to Audrey. "This is my wife, Robin."

Audrey stood and extended her hand. "Mrs. Gregory, it's so nice to meet you. Sorry for the short greeting earlier. I didn't know you were coming by today."

Before Robin could speak, Matt added, "Robin never needs an appointment."

"Understood," Audrey said with a nod. "It's good to finally put a face with the name."

The word finally lodged under Robin's ribs. Why was she just now learning about this assistant? Why was Audrey only now learning about her?

Matt ushered Robin into his office and shut the door.

"An assistant," Robin said as she set the basket of food on his desk.

"The board approved it a few months ago."

"How many months ago?" she asked.

"I hired her in mid-November."

"Yet you've still been working late. How has an assistant helped at all, I wonder," Robin said, her tone sharp.

Matt didn't answer right away. He focused on pulling the sandwiches from the basket. "It's been a transition. I'm still doing a lot myself."

"She could pass for a Victoria's Secret model," Robin said.

"Oh, come on." He paused, registering the hurt on her face. "I don't think I've ever seen you jealous."

"I'm allowed to be a little insecure, especially in this case. It makes me uneasy," she said, grabbing the drinks.

Matt touched her arm lightly. "Hey. Look at me." Their eyes met. "You're the only one I'm with. I thought that was obvious."

She nodded, though it didn't settle much. "I just don't understand why you didn't tell me you hired an assistant."

"I didn't think it was a big deal."

"It is a big deal when you're still staying late. An assistant is supposed to lighten the load," she said.

He let out a breath. "I should have told you. I'm sorry. I wasn't trying to hide anything."

"Maybe start coming home at a decent time now that you've gone public with Audrey," Robin said.

Matt's jaw tightened, but he didn't respond.

The weeks passed, and Matt's long hours continued. Robin's knowledge of the situation caused her to question what might really be going on. She wondered if her husband was having an affair. The entire point of an assistant was to take some of the work off Matt, not cause him to work even more. Her frustrations grew, and the emptiness and doubt consumed her. In her mind, the foundation of their marriage weakened with each passing day.

When Matt was home, Robin did not really talk to him. She stayed in the parlor, consumed by her own work. Avoidance became her defense. She grew colder and more distant, even though part of her hated herself for it.

One afternoon, she looked out the parlor window, distracted by the snow flurries of February. The loneliness and regret reached a peak, and she longed for the companionship of her husband. Her emotions were too heavy, and she began to cry. She didn't realize how loud her sobs were until Matt peeked into the room.

"Robin."

She startled slightly and turned her gaze toward the doorway. She stayed seated, tears still rolling down her cheeks.

He walked in and knelt beside her. "Baby, what's wrong?"

"I'm fine," she said quickly, wiping her face.

"You're not fine," he said gently, brushing his thumb under her eye. "Please don't shut me out."

"I've tried not to, but you've given me no choice," she whispered, avoiding his gaze.

"What does that mean?"

"It's nothing," she said and stood, walking past him.

"Robin, talk to me. We promised each other…"

"When Matt? When should I talk to you? I never see you," she shouted. "You're never here. And when you are, all you do is work."

"You work too," he said automatically. He caught himself, rubbed his forehead, and sighed, frustration simmering. "Do you think I haven't noticed that we barely talk anymore?" His voice rose.

"I don't know what you have or haven't noticed because we don't see each other. You spend more time with your assistant than you spend with me."

"What?" He looked genuinely blindsided. "That's not fair."

"We never spend time together anymore," she cried. "I feel completely alone in this monstrous house. This house that was supposed to be for us."

"Robin, this job was the goal. You know that. I'm fixing a broken system. It takes time. It takes commitment."

"A marriage takes commitment too."

"I'm on probation for a year. You know that. If I screw up, I'm out. Audrey has been helpful."

"I bet."

He stiffened. "That's not what I meant."

"And you act like you're the only one with responsibility," Robin said. "Becoming a supervisor was my goal too, but I didn't devote every waking second of my life to it."

"I made a promise to take care of you," Matt said, a little too defensively. "This job does that. We're financially stable because of it."

"Do you think I care about money? What's the point of any of that if I don't have my husband?" Tears spilled again. "What happens when there's no us? We are falling apart. Don't you see that?"

Robin walked into the dining room and sat on the bench. Matt followed her.

"What do you want me to do?" he asked, his voice raised more from desperation than anger.

"I don't know." She looked up slowly. "You don't even look at me the same. It's like I'm invisible."

"That's not true," he said and sat beside her. "Robin, come on. I do see you."

"No, you don't." Her voice shook. "I don't know what the answer is. I just know we are falling apart. I'm losing you. I don't want a divorce."

"A divorce?" The word rocked him. "Why would you even say that?"

"Because look at us."

"No. I'm not blind. I see we're struggling, but we are not falling apart."

"We are," she said. "Matt, do you know how long it's been since we even had sex? You don't touch me anymore. Do you want to be intimate with me? Or are you getting your needs met somewhere else?"

Infuriated, he stood abruptly. "You think I'm sleeping with Audrey? You actually think that? What the hell, Robin."

"How could I not think it? You didn't tell me about her. You kept her a secret. And she didn't know anything about me either. Why wouldn't you want her? She's beautiful and vibrant. And you don't look at me that way anymore."

Matt dropped his head into his hands for a moment, then lowered himself back beside her.

"What is happening to us?" he said quietly. "We don't fight like this. This isn't us."

"Someone has to compromise," she said. "And if you're cheating on me, just tell me. I can walk away."

"I'm not cheating on you," Matt said firmly. "I would never do that. You know me."

"I don't know you anymore."

He turned toward her, not perfect but desperate. "I'm trying. I really am. From the day I met you, I've been wrapped up in you. I'm not interested in anyone else. You're my wife. My person. But I'm drowning at this job, and I don't know how to balance it. I'm not handling it well. I know that."

Robin swallowed, her voice softening. "Then come home sometimes. I miss you. I miss us."

Matt let out a shaky breath and dropped to his knees in front of her. He held her hands like he was afraid she might disappear. "I hate this. I hate seeing you cry. My chest feels like it's splitting in two. I don't want to lose you."

She leaned into him and he wrapped his arms around her, holding on tighter than necessary, as if trying to anchor them both.

"Nothing is worth losing you," he whispered. "Nothing in this world could take your place. Nothing."

32

The intense exchange between Robin and Matt changed their dynamic. He began coming home by 5:30 p.m. each night. On Fridays he worked half days. To safeguard himself professionally and ease Robin's fears, he hired a second administrative assistant. Stella Bowling was an accomplished woman in her forties with a medical background and a reputation for efficiency. Two assistants meant Matt could focus more on operations during business hours and delegate administrative tasks properly, allowing him to spend less time buried in paperwork after-hours.

The tension between them did not vanish overnight, but the sharpness softened. They were trying, both of them.

It was a lazy Saturday morning in March as snow fell outside the bedroom window. Matt lay awake watching Robin sleep beside him. He reached over and gently touched her hair. Propping himself on his elbow, he leaned in and kissed her cheek.

"Good morning," he whispered.

She smiled softly and stretched. When their eyes met, something loosened inside both of them. The heaviness felt a little lighter.

Matt unbuttoned her pajama top and kissed along her collarbone. They spent the morning wrapped in each other, the quiet intimacy easing some of the strain that had weighed them down for months. They didn't have the right words for the reconciliation they were trying to rebuild, but they could show it.

Afterward, Robin rested on his chest while he stroked her hair. "I love listening to your heartbeat," she murmured.

The moment was peaceful, fragile, warm.

Then the study door slammed repeatedly.

Robin and Matt shot upright. He grabbed his sweats off the floor and Robin pulled on her robe. Together they stepped into the hallway. It was empty, but the framed pictures inside the study rattled violently on the walls.

Matt walked to the study and threw the door open, his pulse loud in his ears. The room was empty.

Behind them, floorboards creaked as though someone was moving toward them. Matt stepped instinctively in front of Robin. Fear flashed through him before anger took over.

"Get out of our house. We're not leaving. This is our home."

The activity stopped as abruptly as it began.

The strange encounter faded into the background. March became April, then May. The trees and flowers around the property bloomed with a beauty that almost hid the darkness simmering beneath their life at Pikeview. But the house never felt completely quiet. Not to Robin.

33

Summer visitation with Olivia began in early June. Her grades had declined further during the spring semester. She seemed more withdrawn each time Robin saw her. Despite their concern, neither she nor Matt pushed. Children retreat for many reasons, and pressing too hard often made things worse.

Robin was working in the flowerbeds when she heard tires crunching on gravel. She looked up as Sheryl's Lexus turned into the lane. The car hadn't fully stopped before Olivia jumped out, slammed the door, and disappeared into the house without a word.

Sheryl stepped out slowly and sighed, rubbing her temples. "God only knows. She's become someone I don't even recognize."

Robin grabbed Olivia's bags from the trunk and carried them inside. She found Olivia sitting on the east porch swing, waiting while Matt finished mowing. Her arms were wrapped tightly around her middle, as if she were holding herself together.

Matt hopped off the tractor, and Olivia ran straight into his arms. She clung to him with a force that startled him.

"Olly, what's wrong?" he asked gently.

"I missed you so much," she whispered. "I'm so glad I get to stay with you all summer."

Robin stood still, studying her trembling shoulders. Something was terribly wrong.

"Are you okay?" Matt asked again, holding her close.

"I just… I can't tell you," Olivia sobbed.

Robin knelt beside them. She brushed tears from Olivia's cheeks, noticing the pallor in her skin and the dark circles beneath her eyes. "You can tell us anything," she said softly.

Olivia looked between them, struggling. Finally, she whispered, "I want to talk to Robin."

Matt nodded. "Alright. I'll finish the yard."

Robin held out her hand. "Let's get something to drink."

Inside the dining room, she poured Kool-Aid and sat with Olivia at the table. Olivia stared into her cup, tapping her fingers rapidly against the glass.

"Tell me what's wrong," Robin encouraged gently.

Olivia hesitated, then blurted, "What does it mean when someone's a virgin?"

Robin kept her expression calm. "Has your mom talked to you about that yet?"

"No. Mom doesn't talk to me about anything. All she does is work."

Before Robin could respond, Olivia's face crumpled and she burst into tears again. Her body language, her appearance, her avoidance. Everything pointed to trauma.

"Honey," Robin said softly, leaning closer, "you've changed so much these last few months. Something serious is going on. Please tell me."

Olivia wiped her cheeks. "Kyle…"

"Kyle is your stepdad, right?"

She nodded.

Robin waited, giving her space.

"He's done things to me that I don't understand."

Robin's stomach tightened, but she stayed steady. "What kinds of things, sweetheart?"

Olivia swallowed hard. "He has different parts. Sometimes he makes me do things to him. Sometimes he does things to me. I tell him no, but he doesn't stop."

Robin's heart cracked, but her training settled over her like instinct. She took Olivia's trembling hands gently.

"Olly," she said softly, "I know this is hard to talk about, but it's important that I ask you something. When was the last time he touched you like that?"

"Just a couple days ago," Olivia whispered. "Everything hurts."

"I'm so sorry, honey." Robin squeezed her hands. "You did nothing wrong. Not one thing. Thank you for telling me. But we need to go to the hospital."

"Why?" she cried, panic rising.

"To make sure your body is okay. I'll be with you the entire time."

"I don't want anyone to know. I'm ugly now," Olivia sobbed. "Kyle said no one will ever love me."

Robin shook her head. "Olly, that's not true. We love you. Nothing will ever change that."

Footsteps approached from the west entrance. Olivia stiffened, fear tightening her small body.

"Don't be afraid," Robin whispered. "You're not alone."

Matt stepped into the doorway. "What's going on?"

Robin nodded toward the stairs. "Olly, why don't you go get your shoes."

Olivia hurried out of the room.

Matt's voice was tight. "Robin. What is happening?"

She walked to him and placed her hands on his shoulders. "Matthew, we need to take Olivia to the hospital. She has been sexually assaulted."

He froze. Then his hand gripped the back of a chair as if he needed to steady himself. "What?"

"You have to stay calm."

"Who did it?"

"Kyle."

Something dangerous flashed across his face. "I'll kill him."

Robin took his face in her palms, grounding him. "Listen to me. She was assaulted recently. Evidence can be collected. But you have to think like a physician right now. She needs you stable."

He swallowed hard, chest heaving as he fought for control. Slowly, he nodded, trying to contain the fire building inside him.

34

When they arrived at Children's Hospital in Dayton, Olivia and Robin went straight to triage while Matt sat in the waiting area. A SANE nurse was paged, and protocol moved quickly. Calls were made to children's services and the sheriff's office. The atmosphere shifted into one Robin knew well professionally, but emotionally, she felt untethered.

Olivia sat on the gurney in a hospital gown, fidgeting with the skin around her cuticles. Robin sat in the chair beside her, trying to appear calm. Matt stood near the wall, arms crossed, jaw tight, trying and failing to mask the storm brewing behind his eyes.

An advocacy worker and a detective entered the room, followed by the SANE nurse. After introductions, they guided Olivia to a child-friendly interview space with a two-way mirror. The detective remained behind the glass. Matt and Robin were escorted back to the waiting area. To Robin's surprise, Olivia didn't cling or argue. She went willingly, with a quiet bravery that broke Robin's heart.

More than an hour passed before the young female detective stepped into the waiting area. "Come with me," she said.

They followed her down a hallway and into a conference room. The physician, SANE nurse, and child advocate sat at the table. Robin and Matt took seats opposite them, hands trembling beneath the surface.

The detective cleared her throat. "Dr. and Mrs. Gregory, Olivia has disclosed consistent sexual abuse beginning at age seven. According to her, Kyle has taken her through multiple stages of sexual activity."

Robin's stomach twisted. Matt stood abruptly and walked to the window, staring out at the Dayton skyline as though the view could steady him. Robin felt tears spilling before she even registered them. Matt pinched the bridge of his nose, his breath uneven.

The detective continued. "An evidence kit has been completed. The prosecutor will be filing charges."

The SANE nurse added, "The fact that we were able to collect physical evidence will strengthen the case."

The detective nodded. "Olivia is very credible. She interviewed clearly, provided detail, and maintained composure. We are securing a warrant now."

"So he'll be arrested today?" Matt asked, turning around. His voice sounded foreign, scraped raw.

"Yes," the detective answered. "The county of jurisdiction will execute it within the next couple of hours."

Robin leaned forward. "Will the recorded interview be enough for prosecution?"

"It should be," the SANE nurse said.

The children's services worker slipped into the room and took a seat.

Matt looked at her. "What happens now?"

"We will be placing Olivia with you under what's called a safety plan," the CPS worker explained. "It allows her to remain in your custody during the investigation and trial."

The detective added, "I strongly recommend filing for full custody."

The advocate spoke next. "Olivia will need outpatient counseling. She doesn't fully understand the impact of what's happened yet. She also disclosed that she believes you, Dr. Gregory, will never forgive her. Family therapy is recommended."

Matt closed his eyes for a moment, then ran a hand through his hair. "I love my little girl," he said quietly, his lip quivering. "This is not her fault. I don't blame her for anything."

"Keep reminding her of that," the SANE nurse said softly.

The advocate slid a business card across the table. "If you need anything, call me, day or night."

"Can we see her now?" Robin asked.

"Yes," the physician said as he stood. "Follow me."

Robin rose, but before they left the room, she turned to Matt and placed her hands firmly on his shoulders. "You have to be strong for her," she said. Her voice didn't waver, even though everything inside her did. "What she needs right now is reassurance. She needs you to hold her and tell her that you still love her. She is terrified that you won't look at her the same way."

"I could never blame her," Matt said.

"I know that. But she doesn't. And this is only the beginning," Robin said gently. "Patience is going to be your greatest virtue right now."

Matt nodded, swallowing hard as the reality of what awaited them settled into his bones.

35

They arrived home around 5:30 p.m. Olivia barely spoke during the drive. The only thing she said was that she wanted to take a bath as soon as they got there. The weight of the hospital still clung to all three of them as they walked through the door.

Robin spent nearly an hour with her in the bathroom. Olivia kept insisting she still did not feel clean.

Matt retreated to the basement, where he pounded the newly hung punching bag until his arms shook. It was the only way he could keep from exploding. His anger burned hot, but he still knew where the line was. Olivia came first.

After helping Olivia wash, Robin got her ready for bed. She sat on the floor with the blow-dryer in her hand, brushing out Olivia's tangled golden hair. Halfway through, Olivia spoke.

"Robin, did I have sex?"

Robin paused just long enough to steady herself. "Is that what he told you?"

"Yes."

"What happened to you isn't sex, sweetheart."

Olivia frowned. "Then what's the difference between what happened to me and what sex is?"

"What happened to you is something you had no control over. You were not given a choice." Robin brushed gently through her hair. "Sex is something shared between two people who both want it. You did not choose this."

Olivia's eyes welled. "I am not a virgin anymore, am I? That is what Gracia said."

Robin's stomach tightened. "Who is Gracia?"

"My stepsister. She is older. She said when Kyle had sex with her, it was the same as with me, and that we are not virgins anymore."

Robin held her composure with effort. "Olly, did you tell the people at the hospital about Gracia?"

"Yes."

"Good." Her voice stayed soft but firm. "Listen to me. Virginity is not something someone takes from you. It is something you choose to give someday, when you are older and safe and with someone you love. You still get to decide that. Does that make sense?"

Olivia nodded.

Robin wrapped her arms around her. "I love you. And I am very proud of you."

"I love you too," Olivia whispered.

The rest of the evening, Robin kept things quiet and simple. She made chicken tenders and French fries. Seeing Olivia eat, even a little, was a relief. Later they curled up on the couch with a movie. By ten o'clock, Olivia was drifting off.

Robin walked her upstairs and tucked her in. Olivia pulled the covers to her chin.

"I want Daddy to tuck me in," she murmured.

"All right. I will go get him."

Robin headed down to the basement. The rhythmic sound of Matt's gloves striking the punching bag echoed through the room. Sweat and raw emotion filled the air.

She stepped in front of him. He finally met her eyes.

"Olivia wants you," she said gently. "She wants you to tuck her in."

Matt stood there breathing hard, hands trembling. He held them out. Robin loosened the Velcro on the gloves.

His eyes were full of doubt and fear. She touched his arm. "It is going to be okay."

"You sure about that?" His voice cracked.

"She is strong. She will come out whole as long as she has us and a good therapist."

Matt clenched his jaw. "I want to wrap my hands around that man's throat and watch the life leave his body."

"I know," Robin said quietly. "I do not blame you. But she will be okay. Look at me. I turned out alright."

Matt froze, eyes widening. "You?"

"I will tell you later," she said softly. "Go see your daughter. I will wait on the porch."

They walked upstairs. Robin continued through the kitchen, then the living room, and finally out onto the porch. She sat on the swing and rested her head against the chain. Memories tried to creep in, old and unwelcome, but therapy had taught her how to breathe through them.

The trees swayed gently under the night sky. Stars glittered like diamonds on black velvet. It was hard to believe such a dreadful day could end in such a quiet moment.

Upstairs, Matt paused outside Olivia's door before stepping inside.

"Hey, baby," he said softly.

"Hi, Daddy."

He sat beside her on the bed.

"Are you mad at me?" she whispered.

"Oh, sweetheart," he said immediately, "of course not. I love you, and nothing will ever change that. What happened to you was not your fault."

"That is what everyone keeps telling me," Olivia said. "So why do I still feel so bad?"

"Because someone hurt you," he said gently. "But you did not do anything wrong."

"That is what Robin said."

"Robin is right." His voice wavered. "I am sorry I did not keep you safe." He stroked her hair. "We love you so much. You know that, right?"

"Yes."

He swallowed hard. "Do you think you can sleep?"

"Can Cookie stay with me?"

"Of course."

He called the dog, who trotted in and curled up beside her.

Matt kissed Olivia's forehead and stepped back. As he left, she pulled the blanket tighter around her.

Emma slipped through the closet door and sat quietly on the floor.

"I am sorry, Olivia," she said without moving her lips.

Olivia nodded. "You were the first person I ever told."

"I am glad you did," Emma replied. "They will keep him from hurting you again. And now you do not have to be scared when the lights go out."

"Thank you for always listening to me," Olivia whispered as her eyes drifted closed.

The room grew still, the old house holding its breath around her.

36

The screen door slammed shut as Matt stepped out onto the east porch. He lowered himself into the space beside Robin, their shoulders almost touching.

"Is she asleep?" Robin asked quietly.

"Yeah," he said.

"She'll be okay as long as she's here with us."

Matt shifted, drawing one leg up beneath him. His voice softened. "What happened to you? Why didn't you ever tell me?"

Robin inhaled slowly and held the breath for a beat before letting it out. "Sexual assault is much more common for young girls than people realize. It's an unfortunate statistic, but it's true." She watched the shadows shift across the field, letting the quiet steady her. "I was twelve. It was my Uncle Simon, my stepdad's brother. He molested me. It only happened once, but once was enough to change everything. I told my parents immediately. They filed charges. He pled out and got five years."

"Five years? That's it?"

"Yep. And he was out in two for good behavior."

Matt shook his head. "What the hell."

"Simon stole my innocence, but I survived it," she said gently. "My mom put me straight into therapy."

Matt reached for her hand. "I'm so sorry."

"Don't be. It was a long time ago, and I'm okay."

They rocked in silence for a moment, the creak of the swing settling around them. Then Matt spoke again, his voice low and his mind spiraling. "Robin... when we've been intimate, have you ever felt apprehensive or uncomfortable because of what happened to you back then?"

"Never," she said without hesitation. "And Olly will be alright. She has us. We'll get her into therapy, and she'll rise above this. She's stronger than she knows."

"I can't imagine what she's feeling," he said, grief tight in his throat. "She trusted him. I trusted him."

"You can't blame yourself. The investigation will run its course. Kyle will likely go to prison, probably longer than Simon did."

The quiet hum of crickets and frogs suddenly disappeared beneath the roar of a car engine tearing up the driveway. Robin and Matt exchanged startled looks. Matt checked his watch.

"Eleven forty-five," he muttered.

He took Robin's hand, and together they walked toward the front of the house. Headlights cut through the darkness as a Lexus shot up the lane. The car braked hard before jerking into park. Sheryl climbed out and ran straight for Matt, throwing her arms around him. Her movements were frantic, almost wild with fear. Robin staggered back, startled.

Matt pushed her away. "What the hell, Sheryl?"

Her face was streaked from crying, shining under the porch light. "I don't know what to do," she sobbed. "They took him down to the station. He swears he didn't do anything to Olly. Why would she make up something so horrible, so vicious?"

"Lie?" Matt snapped. "You think she'd make something like this up?"

"Kyle is a good man," Sheryl insisted.

"No," Robin said firmly. "He's harmed Olly and your stepdaughter."

"Liar!" Sheryl shouted.

"Get the hell out of here," Matt said, pointing down the lane. "I can't do this right now."

"We're her parents, Matt! We should be the ones helping her through this!"

"Jesus Christ, Sheryl. Just leave."

Sheryl turned her fury on Robin. "This is your fault, you little bitch! Filling her head with this crap!" Her voice cracked, desperation spilling into anger.

"Hey, hey!" Matt's posture shifted, instinctively placing himself between them. "You are not going to talk to my wife like that. Robin didn't cause any of this."

Sheryl stumbled, stunned. "You're protecting her? She started all of this!"

"I'm only going to say this once more," Matt said, voice sharp with warning. "Get off my property before I call the police. You've lost your damn mind."

"She put this in Olly's head!" Sheryl screamed. "Can't you see that?"

Matt's expression hardened. "No, she didn't. Your husband chose to hurt our daughter. Where the hell were you?"

"Stop," Robin said softly, stepping between them. "This isn't helping."

"Did he confess?" Matt asked.

"Of course not!" Sheryl shouted. "He didn't do this."

She spun around, stormed back to her car, and peeled out of the driveway, gravel spraying behind her. Robin prayed the noise hadn't woken Olivia. The last thing the girl needed tonight was more instability. She vowed that whatever came next, Olivia wouldn't face it alone.

37

In the days that followed, the house felt heavy and unsettled while everyone tried to recover from the chaos of that night. Even when the rooms were quiet, something in the air felt charged, like the moment before a storm. Everyone moved through the house as if their bodies were heavier than usual. Olivia clung to Robin more, flinching at sudden noises. Matt wasn't sleeping well, and Robin often woke to find him sitting on the edge of the bed, staring into the dark as if waiting for something to happen.

Matt and Robin petitioned for temporary custody of Olivia. Based on the circumstances, the judge graciously granted their request. Eventually, Kyle confessed. He accepted a plea deal for ten years in the state penitentiary. Matt was deeply unsatisfied. Of course, he wanted him to serve more time. Naturally, he wanted revenge. Nothing about the outcome felt like justice, only closure forced upon them by circumstance. He wasn't sure what to do with the anger anymore. It simmered beneath his skin, flaring whenever he thought of Olivia's fear.

Nightmares plagued Olivia. She often woke screaming, begging an unseen force to stop hurting her. The sound of her terror echoed long after she woke, leaving the whole house on edge. Robin and Matt feared she was under spiritual attack. Olivia confessed that Emma was still in the home. However, Emma wasn't a threat, so Robin and Matt accepted her presence. Still, some nights the shadows in the hallway seemed to stretch too far, clinging to the corners in ways that made Robin's skin prickle.

Olivia began her path to healing by engaging in trauma-informed therapy. Family therapy also started. Matt learned to face his guilt. Some days he handled it better than others, but he never stopped trying. Based on the therapist's recommendation, Sheryl was permitted supervised visits. Most of the time, though, Olivia refused to see her mother.

Robin and Matt registered Olivia at her new school. By the end of August, Olivia had started a new chapter in her life. She seemed to be adjusting well as Labor Day came and went. There were still moments when she froze at shadows or startled too easily, but they celebrated every small step forward. Even so, the house still carried an undercurrent of something unspoken, as if a presence watched quietly from the places light didn't reach.

One morning, Robin lay in bed trying to find the motivation to roll out of bed and get dressed for work. She felt physically drained. Finally, she flung her legs over the side and placed her feet on the floor. A rush of nausea overtook her. She ran to the bathroom, lifted the toilet lid, and dropped to her knees. As quickly as the sickness came on, it vanished.

She steadied herself against the sink. For a split second, she felt a cool draft brush the back of her neck, though the window was closed. The sensation passed as quickly as it arrived.

Matt came up the stairs and walked to the bathroom. He leaned against the doorframe. "Feeling under the weather?" he asked with a smirk.

She nodded. "It's probably the flu."

He reached in and felt her forehead. "You don't feel warm." A gleeful smile tugged at his mouth.

"What are you smiling about?" she asked. "How is any of this funny?"

"Are you late starting your period by any chance?"

"Only by a week or so."

Without another word, he walked to the linen closet and pulled out a pregnancy test. Proudly, he held the box up. "I hold in my hand the answer."

"You think I'm pregnant?"

"It's possible. We've been awfully busy working at it. Maybe all that effort has paid off."

He set the box on the sink and headed back downstairs.

Robin stood at the mirror, thoughts racing. A flicker of joy rose in her chest, chased quickly by fear. The timing felt fragile, almost too delicate to trust. Staring down at the box, she wondered if it was possible. She hadn't been on any form of birth control for a few months now. There was only one way to find out.

While she waited for the test result, she got dressed. She put on a pair of beige linen pants and a brown scoop-neck tee. Slipping on some brown flats, she walked back into the bathroom.

Another wave of nausea hit. She took a few deep breaths, waiting for it to pass. Glancing down, she saw the plus sign. A smile spread across her face. She grabbed the test from the sink and hid it behind her back.

As she stepped out of the bathroom, the hallway light flickered once. She paused, frowning, but it held steady when she looked up. She shook her head, blaming exhaustion. She pushed away the unease, reminding herself that trauma played tricks on the senses, blurring the line between what was felt and what was feared.

Matt stood at the island drinking coffee. He wore navy dress pants and brown lace-up shoes. Paired with a white long-sleeved shirt, he had chosen a printed navy tie.

Olivia walked in holding her cereal bowl. She smiled at Matt. "You look good, Daddy."

"Well, thank you."

Robin entered the kitchen with a joyful smile lighting her face.

"Well?" Matt asked anxiously.

"It was positive," she said gently, holding up the test.

"Are you kidding?" His face lit up.

She shook her head, and he rushed to her, scooping her into his arms and spinning her around.

"Ah, I love you," he said, holding the back of her head in his hands.

"We're having a baby!" he shouted.

Olivia jumped up, clapping. "That means I'll be a big sister!"

"Yes!" Robin exclaimed as Matt set her back down.

Beneath her excitement, Olivia's eyes held a flicker of uncertainty, as if she wasn't sure whether this new change might shift the ground beneath her again. Matt held Robin a little longer than necessary, as though anchoring himself to something good before the world could take it away.

The darkness they had lived under for so long finally began to lift with the happy news. Their family was growing, and they couldn't have been more content. For the first time in months, the future felt gentle.

But upstairs, behind the closed door of the spare room, a faint thud echoed against the floorboards, soft enough to ignore, yet loud enough that Robin would remember it later. A faint chill crept up her spine, quick and soft, gone before she could name it.

38

Halloween approached. Olivia wanted to have a Halloween party at the house. She had made several friends at school and wanted them to celebrate with her. As Robin and Olivia stood in the party store, they tried to decide on a theme. Robin wandered through the aisles while Olivia followed behind.

Olivia froze mid-step, her eyes focusing on something Robin couldn't see. She shook her head slightly, lips barely moving. "Not now... I'm busy," she whispered, barely audible. Her fingers tightened around a package of orange balloons, as if grounding herself.

Robin noticed but didn't say anything. Instead, she continued looking at party decorations. Finally, they checked out and headed back home.

In the car, Robin decided to ask. "Who were you talking to back there in the store?"

Olivia's face went pale. She stared out the window, her voice small. "I wasn't talking to anyone. I swear."

"Olly, you don't have to lie to me," she said gently.

The conversation ended without resolution.

The cool November air blew against Robin's skin as she finished one of her nightly walks on the property. She walked in through the west entrance, and the house felt colder than the air outside, a chill she couldn't quite explain. She grabbed a bottle of water from the fridge. Leaning against the sink, she took several long sips.

Olivia walked into the room with a blank stare. "Robin," she began, "something was here in the house."

"What?" Alarm swept through her. For a moment, Robin worried Olivia was blending trauma memories with the spiritual world, but the certainty in the girl's voice told her this was different.

"Something scary was here in the house," Olivia repeated.

"What do you mean, Olly?"

"It was out there on the porch," she said, pointing toward the east entrance. "It was huge. It looked like a shadow. It stared right at me."

Olivia wrapped her arms around herself, as if trying to make her body smaller. The color had drained from her face.

Robin walked through the living room and stepped onto the porch, Olivia trailing behind her. Looking around, Robin didn't see anything out of place. "Is it still here?" she asked.

"Yes."

Robin returned to the couch and lowered herself onto the cushions. Olivia followed without hesitation.

"You can see it, can't you?" Robin asked.

"Yes. I see Emma more and more too. I talk to her all the time now. And today when we were at the party store, a man talked to me. He said he needed help finding his way home. They're just… there. All the time now."

Robin smiled softly and touched Olivia's face. She kept her voice calm, careful not to let her own worry surface. "You have a gift. You don't have to be afraid to talk to me about it. It just shows how special you are."

"But the big scary thing... I don't like it."

"It's still here?" Robin asked.

Olivia nodded and stood up, holding out her hand. Robin took it, and they walked to the screen door. Olivia pointed to the far-right rocking chair. "It's standing right there."

Robin pushed open the door and walked to the chair. She stood behind it. "Here?" she asked.

"Yes. It's looking right at you."

"Is it saying anything?"

"It just growls a lot," Olivia answered.

"Does it look like a person?" Robin asked.

"No. I can't see its face. It looks like it's wearing a hood."

A few silent moments passed. "It's gone," Olivia said calmly.

Robin returned to the couch again, trying to steady her breath. Olivia joined her.

"Olivia, do you understand what is happening?"

"Kind of," she said with a shrug.

"What do you think is happening?"

"Well, I can see things no one else can. Emma. The lady in the field. The man in the tuxedo. They can all talk to me."

"Has Emma mentioned seeing a light?" Robin asked.

"She said there's one sometimes, but then it gets farther and farther away. Is that where we go when we die?"

"I think we live somewhere different when we die," Robin said. "Sometimes we can still talk to people here after we leave. We might need help to do it, but I think that might be where your abilities come in."

"What do you mean?" Olivia asked.

"Some people can see and hear things others can't. And you might be one of them."

"What's that called?"

"A medium can see the dead. They can talk to them and even help them. It's a gift not everyone has. Do the things you see scare you?"

"Not really. Most of the spirits are really nice. I see them everywhere we go."

"I can teach you how to navigate all of this if you want me to," Robin offered.

"That would be great." Olivia's face lit up.

"There are spirit guides who can help keep you safe, especially when you're talking to the spirits."

"Wow," Olivia breathed. "That would be awesome."

Robin took time each day to help Olivia understand her gift. Sometimes they meditated. Other times they researched or simply talked. They walked the property searching for lost spirits and occasionally visited the local cemetery where Olivia could focus and tune in to her abilities.

Neither Robin nor Olivia mentioned any of this to Matt. As much as Robin wanted to discuss things with him, she knew he wouldn't understand. Olivia needed encouragement and guidance, not doubt. For now, the truth had to stay between them. Olivia's safety depended on keeping this world small, quiet, and protected. Robin only hoped she could contain what she didn't fully understand.

39

One evening, Robin stood looking out the window at the east field. She rubbed the small bump protruding from her abdomen. A sudden wave of uneasiness washed over her. She wondered if it was just pregnancy jitters.

The rocking chair on the porch caught her attention. It moved gently on its own, rocking back and forth, and Robin knew she wasn't alone. In her mind's eye, she saw the woman from her dream. She decided to test the space between them, to see if communication was possible.

"I know you're here," she whispered.

A familiar sadness settled over her shoulders like a heavy shawl. Then, as quickly as it came, the energy shifted, darker now, heavier, unmistakably uncomfortable. The darkness pressed in a little too close, and for the first time, Robin felt genuinely unsafe in her own home. A chill unraveled down her spine, settling low in her stomach like a warning she couldn't ignore.

Robin narrowed her gaze and set her jaw. "I know what you are," she murmured.

It was time to research the origins of Pikeview. She had put it off long enough, avoiding it, really. A part of her didn't want to uncover what had happened on the property or in the house. But she knew she needed answers.

She walked carefully down the basement steps. Matt was punching the heavy bag hanging from the ceiling. Sweat soaked his hair as his fists slammed rhythmically into the leather.

Robin folded her arms. "I'm going to research the house on Monday," she announced.

Matt stopped and steadied the bag. He wiped his forearm across his brow, breathing hard as he tried to read her expression. "Oh? What happened?"

"It's just time," she said. "The emotional swings… they're too much some days. I want to find out why I'm feeling what I'm feeling."

"Don't you think it could be the pregnancy?"

"Some of it, sure. But I think there are other connections too."

"I thought things were better," he said, walking to the futon and sitting down. Robin followed.

"Things are better. But Olivia has been seeing things. And I'm fairly certain she saw the entity that's attached to this house."

Shock moved through Matt, erasing the color from his face. "She saw what?" His voice cracked, fear slipping beneath the anger.

"I didn't want to overwhelm you with it," Robin said, picking at her cuticles. "I know how much you struggle with all of this."

"My daughter is seeing a demon? Did I hear that correctly?"

"I'm sorry I didn't say something sooner."

Matt's face tightened and he shook his head in frustration. "I swear it feels like I'm in a science fiction movie. None of this has ever made sense to me."

"I know," Robin said gently as she stood. "I know how hard it is for you to believe."

"I've tried to believe. I've tried to be open-minded. Even your dad talked to me about some of this. But a demon? Robin, that sounds impossible."

"It's the only explanation that makes sense for what Olivia described. And if my nightmares are any indication, terrible things happened here long before we arrived."

Later that night, Matt lay in bed staring up at the ceiling. Once again, he struggled to settle his thoughts and find sleep. His apprehension and cynicism were being challenged by so many things. His mind felt heavy and cluttered. He rolled his wedding band around on his finger as he realized that the primary issue was that his own belief system was being challenged.

The temperature in the room rapidly changed. It grew colder. He looked over at Robin as she slept. She gathered the covers up and nestled into them, her unconscious body seeking warmth. He watched as her breath came out in a mist. He looked down and realized he could also see his own breath.

He looked at the doorway. A tall, dark figure floated there. He watched as the black mist entered the room and stood at the end of Robin's side of the bed. Matt was paralyzed by fear, and his hands felt as if they were chained to the bed.

He watched helplessly as the entity pulled the covers off of Robin, exposing her bare legs. Depressions in her skin appeared as the entity touched her. Matt wanted to protect her. He wanted to scream, but nothing came out.

Robin stirred and reached for the covers, pulling them back over her body. Again, the entity yanked them away. Matt watched in horror as the presence pressed against her, its cold, invisible hands sliding across her chest and tugging at the waistband of her pajama pants.

She shifted again. "Matt… stop," she murmured, her voice groggy.

Suddenly, three bloody scratch marks appeared on her shin, and she shot upright in bed. She fumbled for the lamp and switched it on. Matt gasped beside her and jerked upright as if he had been held underwater. He leaned forward, dragging air into his lungs.

"Are you okay?" she asked, placing a trembling hand on his back.

He nodded weakly and swung his legs out from under the covers. His feet hit the floor, and he made his way to the bathroom for the first aid kit. When he returned, he sat heavily on the edge of the bed, still shaken.

"What just happened?" she whispered.

"I do not even know how to explain what I saw," Matt said as he opened the kit.

"It was here, wasn't it? You saw it."

He nodded, his expression bleak. "It scratched you. It touched you. It tried to take off your clothes. And I could not move. I could not do anything."

Matt lowered his head into his hands. Robin moved closer and sat beside him. "We are going to figure this out, Matt. I promise. We will."

40

Robin and Matt sat waiting as the historian searched the back room for Pikeview records. The hum of the overhead lights filled the silence. Robin drummed her fingers on the table before finally sighing. They had already been waiting longer than she expected, and she wondered just how much documentation Pikeview had accumulated over the years.

At last, the older woman reappeared carrying a very large box. She set it down with a soft grunt, then disappeared again. When she returned, she carried a leather-bound volume swollen with old newspapers. She stepped out once more and came back with several stacks of loose papers, yellowed with age. Wiping her hands on her skirt, she excused herself, leaving Robin and Matt facing a mountain of history.

They exchanged a look before beginning to sift through the contents. The paper smelled of dust, mildew, and something older than both of them could name. Matt tried to remind himself to stay grounded in facts, but even he could feel a quiet unease settling in as they uncovered more.

Matt froze, his mouth parting slightly.

Robin's pulse picked up. "What is it?"

He lifted a fragile clipping dated March 1870. "Listen to this. The headline says, 'Local Butler Suspected of Murder'." He cleared his throat and continued reading: "Mr. Michael Sims was arrested today on suspicion of murder. Sources say Mr. Sims participated in unsavory acts with runaway girls. He assisted a local doctor with several operations resulting in the deaths of numerous young women. Sims refuses to reveal the whereabouts of the mastermind behind the operations and remains in the county jail without bond."

Robin felt a chill crawl along her spine as a memory surfaced. The dream she had shortly after they moved in. The woman on the table. The two men hovering over her. The helplessness.

Her eyes met Matt's. "Is there more?"

He swallowed and nodded. "Here's another one. Dated a month later." He read slowly, his voice tightening. "Michael Sims escaped from the county jail. Authorities initiated a manhunt but were unable to find him. He was considered armed and dangerous. Then... here." Matt pulled a second clipping from beneath the first. "It says Sims was later discovered dead at Pikeview Manor. He hung himself in the basement."

Robin pressed her hand to her throat, her breath catching. "I felt that," she whispered. "In the basement. The pressure. The weight. I thought it was my imagination."

Matt continued reading, his brow furrowed. "It also says Sims was responsible for killing several young women at Pikeview. This place must have been... some kind of hidden clinic."

"Or a hunting ground," Robin murmured. "It sounds like Sims wasn't working alone. Like he was part of a serial killing team."

Matt's expression shifted so drastically that Robin leaned forward. "Matt? What is it?"

He lifted a brittle photograph, his fingers trembling. "This woman... she's the same woman I've seen in the field."

Robin's heart pounded in her ears. "I've seen her too. She's been in my dreams. And I saw her in the field the night we were unpacking."

Matt stared at the photo. "How is this even possible?"

"It might be that some of the victims crossed over, and some didn't," Robin said. Her voice was quiet, but steady.

"Crossed over?"

"Some spirits leave this world peacefully. Others don't. When someone dies violently, they might not even realize they're dead. They could wander, confused, stuck between worlds."

Matt drew in a shaky breath. "What about Emma?"

Robin shuffled through the papers until she found another clipping. "Here. This says that our house was once owned by a Mr. and Mrs. William Cleary. Their daughter, Emma, died after falling down the stairs. She broke her neck."

Robin hesitated, staring at the article. "I dreamt that exact thing. I was chasing a ball down the stairs. I slipped. I fell. I knew I had died." She pressed her fingers to her temple. "They've been trying to communicate with me from the start." She handed Matt the clipping. "Look at her picture."

Matt studied it. A little girl with dark hair and a ribbon stared back, the expression hauntingly familiar. "She looks exactly like Olivia described." He exhaled slowly. "Does it say when she died?"

"June 1868," Robin replied. "Sims was working for the family then. According to these records, after Emma's death, her parents moved away and left Sims in charge. He eventually purchased the home."

Matt leaned back, stunned. "So let me get this straight. A little girl died in the house. Multiple women were murdered there. The butler hung himself in the basement. How is this not the plot of a horror movie? It sounds insane."

"It's documented, Matt. Not just here, but through multiple sources." Robin swept her hand over the piles of clippings and records. "This is real."

Matt rifled through another stack. "Here's something else. Property maps say there's a cemetery on the land. It's marked near the back of the property line. Have you ever seen graves back there?"

Robin shook her head. "I've never explored the woods. Have you?"

"No," he admitted. "But maybe we should."

Robin lifted another brittle page. As her eyes scanned the text, her mouth dropped open. "Matthew," she whispered, bringing her hand to her mouth. "Our house served as the county morgue in the mid-1900s. The basement was used as an autopsy room."

Matt let out a humorless laugh. "Unbelievable. It just keeps getting better."

"Wait. There's more." She pulled another article closer. "This headline says, 'Pikeview Manor Said to Be Haunted.' After the morgue moved across town, the Rawlins family lived there for five years. The wife, Sophia Rawlins, died during childbirth. Then another family moved in around 1938 but left within three years."

Robin flipped through several more clippings. "It's the same story over and over. Families move in. Families move out. Never more than five years. The O'Bryans told us it sat empty for at least twelve years before we bought it."

Matt exhaled through his nose. "No wonder."

"And look at this," she said. "In 1980, a woman named Ginger Morgan reported hearing voices, seeing apparitions, and encountering a child who claimed to have died there in the late 1800s."

"Emma," Matt said softly.

"Ginger also heard objects moving, appliances turning on by themselves, and screams coming from the basement."

Matt ran a hand through his hair. "Some of that hasn't happened to us. Thank God."

"Maybe it won't," Robin said, though she didn't sound convinced.

"Or maybe we've been too distracted to notice," Matt replied quietly.

The weight of everything settled over them. Generations of tragedy. Layers of death. Voices reaching through time. The house had been calling out long before they arrived.

And now, they had no choice but to face the truth: Pikeview Manor was not just haunted. It was saturated with the dead.

41

Matt and Robin returned home, the weight of Pikeview's past lingering between them. For the first time since moving in, the strange events had context. A name. A history. Answers. And although the truth was horrifying, the clarity made the house feel slightly less threatening. At least the unknown now had an identity.

Matt pulled up to the west entrance and waited while Robin climbed out. He headed toward town to pick up Olivia from her friend's house, leaving Robin alone with her thoughts. She walked upstairs to the study and eased herself into Matt's desk chair, letting the quiet settle around her.

The peace lasted only seconds.

A sudden and violent pounding erupted from inside the walls. The blows were so deep and hollow that they seemed to vibrate through the floorboards. Robin froze. Instinct begged her to flee, but a stronger impulse rose inside her. She was tired of being intimidated. Tired of feeling outmatched in her own home.

The pounding intensified, rhythmic and deliberate, as if responding to the shift in her energy. The hair on her arms lifted.

Robin rose slowly and faced the wall. "We both know what you are," she whispered. "You don't belong here. You need to leave."

A burst of freezing air slammed into her. It stole the breath from her lungs. Her hair lifted as though caught in an unseen current. She gasped and turned to the computer screen.

In the dark reflection behind her stood a towering, hooded figure. It was enormous, easily seven and a half feet tall, and its shape seemed to drink in the light around it.

Robin swallowed hard. Trembling, she squared her shoulders.

"This is our house," she said firmly. "Get out."

A surge of strength rolled through her, surprising and unfamiliar. Just as quickly as it came, it faded, leaving her breathless and shaky.

She spun, expecting the figure behind her.

The room was empty.

A moment later, the west entrance slammed with enough force to rattle the walls. The sound jolted her, but when she heard Matt and Olivia downstairs, adrenaline turned to urgency.

"I need Olly!" she called.

"What's wrong?" Matt shouted.

"Just bring her up here!"

Footsteps pounded up the stairs. Olivia entered first with Matt close behind. The instant she crossed the threshold, an icy wave engulfed her. Her cheeks flushed from the cold. Her breath puffed visibly.

Matt stopped short, stunned. His face paled, and he looked between Robin and the frigid air as though his skepticism had finally cracked.

Robin crouched to Olivia's height. "Olivia, tell me what you see. Tell me what you feel."

Olivia scanned the room, her expression tightening. "I don't see anything… but I feel anger. Something's really mad at you." She paused, frowning. "I do see what it is, though."

Robin's pulse quickened. "Olly, where's Emma? Is she in the house?"

Olivia shook her head. "No. She's outside. She's too scared to come in. She said she won't step inside as long as the bad one's here. It scares her."

Robin's heart clenched. "That was good, Olly. Very good. You did great."

Olivia looked up at her. "Can I go now?"

"Yes," Robin whispered.

The moment Olivia stepped into the hallway, the cold lifted. The study felt lighter, almost relieved.

Matt remained rooted in place, disbelief and fear warring in his expression.

Robin brushed past him and headed downstairs. He followed quickly.

"What's going on?" he demanded. His voice was tight, cracking at the edges.

Robin told him everything. The pounding. The cold blast. The towering figure reflected behind her. The confrontation she had forced herself to stand through.

Matt blinked repeatedly, like he was trying to force rationality back into place. "I still don't understand why you asked for Olivia."

Robin hesitated. "I can't explain right now."

His frustration rose quickly. "Robin, Olivia's my daughter!"

"You wouldn't believe me if I told you."

"Try me."

Robin motioned for him to sit beside her. "Olly is extraordinary. She's sensitive to things you and I can't see. Things you've tried very hard not to believe in."

Matt rubbed both hands over his face, his denial visibly slipping. "Jesus. Why am I not surprised."

He stood abruptly and pulled Robin to her feet. "We're taking a walk. Put on a jacket."

Robin slipped away, grabbed a windbreaker, and followed him outside. They headed toward the woods behind the house. The cool air calmed neither of them.

"Do you remember the map?" Matt asked, voice strained. "The cemetery. Where is it supposed to be?"

Robin pointed deeper into the trees. "Somewhere over that way."

They walked through the underbrush in tense silence. Sunlight filtered through the canopy in narrow beams. Then Robin stopped.

Five gravestones leaned in a small clearing. A rusted iron fence surrounded them. Moss crept along the bases of the stones, nature reclaiming forgotten lives.

Robin counted quietly. "Five."

Matt took photos, then pushed open the gate and stepped inside. Kneeling, he read, "Virginia Cleary. Martin Cleary. Leon Cleary."

"It's this one," Robin said softly, touching a stone topped with a carved lamb. "Emma's."

Matt read the inscription. "Our angel, Emma Elaine Cleary."

Robin's throat tightened. "How sad."

Before either of them could speak, a scream tore through the woods. It was sharp, terrifying, unmistakably real.

They locked eyes, then sprinted toward the house.

Another scream erupted as they reached the porch. They burst through the east door and skidded into the kitchen.

Olivia stood against the counter, trembling violently.

Matt rushed to her. "What's wrong? Are you hurt?"

Tears streaked down her face. "I saw it," she cried.

Matt scanned the room desperately. "What did you see?"

"It talked to me," Olivia sobbed. "It told me it hates Robin. It hates the baby." Her voice cracked. "It said it wants Robin to bleed like the others."

Her knees gave out. Matt caught her, wrapping her in his arms as she sobbed against him. He kissed her cheeks and murmured, "You're safe. I've got you. Nothing is going to hurt you."

Robin got a bottle of water from the fridge and knelt beside them, stroking Olivia's hair. "It's alright, sweetheart. You're safe."

Olivia clung to Matt. "I don't want anything to happen to you."

Robin met her eyes. "Nothing will happen to me," she whispered. "I promise."

42

After setting up an air mattress and sleeping bag, Matt and Robin settled into bed with their books, waiting for Olivia to fall asleep. Once her breathing deepened, they slipped quietly downstairs and curled up on the living room couch. The television murmured in the background, more for comfort than entertainment.

Matt leaned forward, elbows on his knees. His voice was low and heavy. "I'm not sure how much longer I can do this."

Robin closed her book. "What do you want to do? Whatever you say, I'll support."

"I want to understand what's happening with my daughter."

"She's clairvoyant," Robin said gently. "There's no question anymore."

Matt let out a hollow laugh. "But how? How can she see and know these things?"

"It's a gift," Robin replied with a small shrug. "One she's always had."

"It feels more like a curse," he snapped, the words spilling out before he could stop them. "How could you let her get involved in this? This is too much for a kid."

Robin's expression tightened. "I didn't do anything to her. This didn't come from me. She's always seen Emma, long before I came into the picture. You said it yourself. And after what she went through... sometimes trauma intensifies things a child already carries. It doesn't create the gift. It amplifies it." She paused, her tone softening. "You should be proud of her, Matt. She's incredibly brave, and she's trying to understand something most adults couldn't handle."

Matt dragged a shaky hand through his hair. The frustration radiating off him filled the room. "This just keeps getting more bizarre. Every time I think we've reached the limit, something else happens."

"I'm sorry you're upset," Robin whispered. His anger wasn't aimed at her, but she felt the sting all the same.

Matt looked at her, his voice wavering between disbelief and exhaustion. "Everything you've told me, everything we've seen… it's all rooted in mysticism. Spirits. Light. Darkness. It sounds made up."

"But you've seen it," Robin reminded him quietly.

Matt looked away. "I know. And I still think logic has to win at some point. That's how I'm wired. I don't want Olivia to deal with things she shouldn't have to. Not at her age."

Robin softened again. "Faith doesn't require understanding. It just asks you to stay open. Children often have abilities because they haven't learned to shut out what they see. They're closer to the light. They trust their experiences."

Matt shook his head slowly. "I don't know if I believe in anything. I never have. And this is challenging me in ways you can't imagine."

Robin reached out a hand. "Let me see your phone."

He hesitated. "Why?"

"You took pictures in the woods today. Maybe they'll help."

Matt unlocked his phone and handed it to her. They sat shoulder to shoulder as they scrolled through the images together.

The first few were ordinary. Then the next ones appeared.

Small white orbs hovered in midair. A swirl of mist drifted beside a tombstone. Another photo revealed a faint, childlike figure standing near the grave marker with a bright red bow in her hair.

Emma.

Matt's breath hitched.

But the final image made both of them go still.

Behind Emma, several feet back, loomed a massive dark figure, suspended above the ground. It had no features, no eyes or limbs, only a shape that radiated something cold and ancient.

Matt's thumb trembled against the phone.

Robin touched his arm. "Save these, Matt. All of them. They're going to be important."

Matt didn't speak. He only stared at the screen, swallowing hard as the truth pressed in from every direction.

For the first time, logic had nowhere left to go.

44

The room was dark, so dark that Robin could not tell whether walls surrounded her or whether she stood in a space that had no boundaries at all. A single cone of light shone on a man seated at a small, gleaming metal table. His back faced her. Everything beyond him was swallowed in a quiet, suffocating blackness.

Robin stepped closer. Her feet echoed faintly, as though she walked across a surface far larger than the room should have allowed. She felt the darkness tighten around her like a closing hand.

When she reached the table and stepped in front of him, she stopped cold.

It was Matt.

His complexion was ashen, drained of life, but his eyes still held the familiar glimmer she knew by heart. Shadows drifted over his face, shifting like something alive.

Then she saw movement.

Long, black, skeletal fingers emerged behind him. They threaded through his hair, gripping and twisting. The tips pressed into his skull, slipping beneath the skin as though the bone offered no resistance at all.

Matt's eyes lifted toward her.

Then they turned entirely black.

Robin tried to call his name, but her voice would not rise. Her throat locked. Air thinned. Panic prickled beneath her skin. She reached toward him, but her hand stopped short, as if the dream itself refused to let her touch him. She stumbled backward, gasping for a breath she could not fully take.

A door appeared to her right. It glowed softly as thin bands of light pushed through its cracks, warm and inviting in the middle of the void.

Drawn to it, she placed her trembling hand on the knob and pulled.

The woman from her earlier dreams stood inside. Pale dress. Dark hair. Haunted eyes. The same woman she had seen in the east field. Her presence radiated desperation.

"You must help us," the woman said, her voice trembling. A faint echo twisted her words, as if others whispered with her.

Robin shook her head helplessly. "I have tried."

"You have to help us," the woman cried, her voice breaking apart. "He grows stronger. He has taken so many."

The last words hit Robin like a physical blow.

She jolted upright in bed; her breath caught in her throat. Sweat cooled on her skin.

Matt stirred and turned on the lamp. Warm light softened the shadows.

"Another dream?" he asked, rubbing his eyes.

Robin nodded, still trying to steady her breathing.

"Come here," he murmured as he sank back against the pillows and opened his arms.

She curled against him and pressed her ear to his chest. The steady rhythm of his heartbeat grounded her. Slowly, her breathing slowed. The shadows in her mind faded just enough for sleep to pull her under again.

45

After working all day, Robin came home through the snow and ice. January marked five months of her pregnancy, and the soft flutters of movement in her womb always made her smile. The warmth of the house contrasted sharply with the winter air, but something about the stillness felt off as she walked upstairs to change.

She slipped into her thin cotton gown and stood before the antique oval mirror. Turning sideways, she cupped the small curve of her belly.

Matt walked in holding a book, dressed in flannel pajamas. Whatever he had planned disappeared the moment he saw her. He crossed the room, knelt, and rested a gentle hand on her belly before kissing it.

"Love you so much, little one," he whispered.

Warmth settled in her chest. Robin brushed her fingers through his hair, noticing new strands of gray. A soft smile touched her lips as he rose to meet her eyes.

The memory of last night's dream flickered through her mind, but she pushed it away. She wanted to hold on to this calm.

"Are you ready for bed?" she asked.

"I am. It has been a long day," he said with a tired breath.

They climbed into bed and settled together, Matt's arm wrapped securely around her. Within minutes, sleep pulled them under.

Robin woke with a violent gasp.

Her hands flew to her throat. Panic surged as she fought for air. Her vision blurred with tears. A cold, crushing weight pressed against her neck.

Above her, a black mist rippled, twisting like smoke caught in a current she could not escape. It pulsed once, as if acknowledging her terror.

Her mouth opened to scream, but no sound came out.

Matt jerked awake. For a split second he froze, disoriented, then scrambled upright. He reached for the lamp, knocking something off the nightstand in the process before flooding the room with light. He saw nothing above her, but the terror on her face sent fear shooting through him.

"Robin?" His voice shook as he dropped to his knees beside the bed. "Robin, please talk to me. Can you hear me?"

The invisible pressure around her throat tightened. Robin kicked violently, her lungs burning as she clawed at her neck. Her body fought against a force only she could feel.

Matt reached toward her but hesitated, terrified of hurting her. "Tell me what to do. Please tell me what to do."

Just when her strength faltered, the pressure vanished.

Air rushed into her lungs. She sat upright, coughing hard, tears streaming down her face as she held her throat.

Matt gripped her shoulders, his hands trembling. "What happened? What happened to you?" His voice wavered between fear and anger, as if unsure who or what he was supposed to blame.

"It tried to kill me," she managed between coughs.

Matt pulled her into his chest but could not steady his breathing. "I am right here. Breathe with me. Just breathe." His hand trembled against her back.

She shook uncontrollably. "I could not breathe. It was choking me."

"Were you dreaming?" he asked, though he already feared the answer.

"No," she whispered. "I was awake."

Exhaustion weighed her down as she leaned back against the pillows, her hand still guarding her throat.

Matt stood there for a moment, unsure of what to do. Then his expression twisted in alarm. "Robin. Go look at your neck. Please."

Confused, she stood and crossed to the mirror.

Her breath caught.

Bruises were already forming along her throat. Scratches cut across the skin. As she watched, a pattern deepened, unmistakable and horrifying.

Rope.

Her knees weakened.

She returned to bed and sat beside Matt, her voice trembling. "This is getting worse. I am trying to stay strong, but I cannot fight something like this. I cannot defend myself."

Matt reached for her but stopped short, as if afraid his touch might hurt her. His voice cracked. "I do not know how to fix this. I hate that I cannot fix this."

He brushed her hair aside to look at the injury again. The marks were darkening. The rope imprint grew more defined, tightening even after the attack had ended.

There was no denying it now.

Something had attacked her.

Matt exhaled shakily. He raked a hand through his hair, pacing once before sinking onto the edge of the bed. Fear settled into his bones. He looked at her, helpless, and already thinking of what they would have to do next.

46

After the disturbing incident of that evening, Robin and Matt did their best to move forward. Saturday arrived clear and cold, sunlight glittering across the snow. Inside the house, everything felt unusually quiet. Olivia was staying with the O'Bryans, and Matt was outside shoveling the driveway.

Robin folded laundry upstairs, moving from room to room as she put things away. She had lost count of how many times she had carried baskets up and down the stairs. This time she carried a full basket of towels. She knelt at the linen closet and began stacking them neatly on the shelves.

Movement flickered at the edge of her vision.

She turned toward the staircase, expecting to see Matt or Olivia. No one was there. She brushed it off and went back to her task. A moment later, the floorboards at the landing creaked softly; that familiar sound of old wood shifting beneath small, careful footsteps.

Robin paused. "Emma?" she asked gently.

She had not seen the little girl lately, but she often sensed her nearby, watching from the periphery of their lives as though longing to belong.

To settle her own nerves, she murmured, "Olivia's at the neighbors today. She'll be home later."

Downstairs, the kitchen door slammed. She heard Matt kick off his boots into the tray by the door. A small smile tugged at her lips. "That's Matt coming in from the cold," she whispered to the empty hallway. "Should we go say hello?"

The temperature dropped instantly.

A cloud of white breath escaped her lips. The cold was sharp, sudden, and wrong. She forced herself to think rationally. The furnace might be struggling, the fireplaces unlit, maybe a duct was blocked.

She called down the stairs, "Matt, I think the furnace needs checked. It's freezing up here."

"I'll look in a minute," he answered from the kitchen.

Robin finished with the towels, lifted the empty basket, and walked toward the staircase. She stepped onto the first stair, then the second and third. As she placed her foot on the fourth step, something shoved her hard between the shoulder blades.

Two hands. Firm. Deliberate.

The basket flew from her grip. Robin pitched forward. Her body slammed against the stairs. Her head struck wood once, then again, pain detonating behind her eyes as she tumbled past the landing and into the hallway below.

She lay face down, stunned. The world tilted sharply and began to dim. She tried to push herself up, but her arms trembled and gave out. Darkness swept over her like a tide.

When she opened her eyes again, a piercing beeping filled her ears. Harsh fluorescent light pressed against her vision. Confusion muddied everything as she fought to understand where she was. A warm hand held hers.

Matt.

He sat beside the hospital bed, eyes swollen and red. She felt a bandage wrapped around her head. Her mouth was dry, her throat thick.

"Hey, baby," he whispered. "How are you feeling?"

She blinked. "Where am I?"

He exhaled shakily. "You're in the hospital. You took a bad fall."

"Why? What happened?" She rubbed the ache pulsing at her temple.

Matt swallowed hard. "Robin… what do you remember?"

She searched her memory. "I had the empty basket. I was taking it downstairs. I remember… someone shoved me. Then I fell. I think." Her eyes lifted to his. "Did I fall?"

"You did," he said softly. A tear slid down his cheek. "You hit your head. You have a concussion, but no broken bones."

Robin's hand moved instinctively to her abdomen.

Her belly was flat.

Her breath caught.

"No." The word scraped out of her. "No… no, no." Panic sharpened her voice. "Where is my baby? Matt… where is my baby?"

Matt's grip tightened around her hand. Tears spilled freely down his face. For a long moment he couldn't speak.

"Matt," she begged, her voice breaking. "Please. Where is my baby?"

He closed his eyes. When he finally spoke, his voice was barely a whisper. "They did everything they could. There was too much bleeding… too much trauma." His throat tightened. "The baby couldn't be saved."

The words crushed her.

Her body trembled uncontrollably.

"A son?" she whispered, needing something, anything to anchor herself.

Matt nodded. "Yes."

He lifted her hand to his lips and cried into it. Robin broke with him, their grief folding together, heavy and raw. The reality settled in like ice: they would be leaving the hospital without their child.

The rest of the day blurred. After a sedative, Robin slept deeply and didn't fully wake until halfway through the next afternoon. When she opened her eyes, Matt stood looking out the window. She couldn't tell which wing of the hospital they were in, nor did it matter.

Later, as they discussed funeral arrangements, they chose to give their son a proper burial. They named him Bryan Garrett. Because of Robin's fragile condition, Doris and Amy went with Matt to the funeral home to choose a casket.

Over the next several days, Robin drifted in and out of sedation. When she finally refused her medication, clarity came in slow, aching waves. She found herself standing at the window of the master bedroom.

She turned toward the oval mirror.

Her hands traced the still slightly swollen curve of her abdomen.

The emptiness hit her like a physical blow. The flutters were gone. The promise of life gone. The entity had taken what she loved most.

Anger rose, raw and consuming.

Tears fell onto the floor. In the silence, she sensed the woman from her dreams standing behind her, quiet, watchful, grieving with her.

Robin pressed her palm to her stomach and wondered if she would ever feel whole again.

47

The church was filled to capacity as Robin and Matt sat in the front pew. Friends and family crowded the sanctuary, the air thick with quiet sympathy and grief. Robin kept her gaze fixed on the tiny casket at the front of the altar. Everything else blurred into muted shapes and color.

Richard stepped up to the pulpit. He took a long breath to steady himself. "Please join me in prayer."

Robin didn't close her eyes. She couldn't. Her attention stayed on Bryan's casket.

"Our loving Father in Heaven," Richard began, his voice trembling despite his effort to keep it steady. "We come with heavy hearts today. We ask for the peace that only You can give. We are confused, Lord, so help us find understanding and healing in this shadowy time. We ask this in Jesus' name, Amen."

He looked at Robin and Matt before turning back to the casket.

"It's never easy to accept the death of someone young... especially a baby," he said softly. "I once heard a saying: when we lose our parents, we lose our past. When we lose a spouse, we lose our present. But when we lose a child... we lose our future."

He paused, emotion tightening his features. "As a grandfather, I feel that deeply today."

He continued, "In the book of James, we're reminded that we don't know what tomorrow will bring. Our life is just a vapor that vanishes away." He lifted his hand, making a faint, wispy gesture. "Life is short, but it matters deeply to God."

His southern accent thickened as he spoke. "Ecclesiastes says, 'He has made everything beautiful in its time. He has also set eternity in the hearts of men, yet they cannot fathom what God has done from beginning to end.'"

Richard's voice faltered for a moment. He blinked and met Robin's eyes. "Robin believes that this mortal body holds us captive, and that when we shed the confines of this flesh, that's when we are finally free. And today, we can take heart knowing that little Bryan is free… and he is rejoicing with the angels and with our Heavenly Father."

The congregation sang a final hymn—soft, wavering, deeply felt. When the last note faded, the funeral director gently ushered everyone out, leaving Robin and Matt alone with their son.

Robin rose slowly and walked toward the casket. Matt stayed close, his arm around her waist. She stared down at Bryan's tiny still face. She brushed her fingertips along the soft blue lining, memorizing every detail. He wore a blue footed sleeper. He looked like he should wake up. Like he should stretch or cry.

But he didn't.

He never would.

Robin reached in and smoothed a small curl from his forehead. Her gaze drifted to the size of the casket.

"Look at this," she whispered. "It's the size of a shoebox." Her voice broke. She traced the polished wood. "He'll be so cold in the ground."

Matt's breath shuddered. He reached in and touched Bryan's hand, barely bigger than his thumb. "You'll always be remembered," he said softly before leaning down to kiss their son's forehead.

Robin's voice splintered. "Goodbye, little one," she whispered. "I'm so sorry."

48

After the funeral, days passed into weeks and then into months. Robin took a leave of absence from work. She slept most of the time, trying desperately to escape the reality of the loss. She barely ate. With the shades drawn, she hid from every living thing. She wanted to be dead, too. She wanted to be with her son. She knew that wherever he was had to be beautiful. He was not in pain. He was free and at peace. Robin, on the other hand, lived in a hell unlike anything she had ever known. Even her joints ached from the weight of carrying so much sorrow.

While Robin fought her battle with grief and depression, Matt struggled to find his footing as well. His anger outweighed his sadness. He thought that maybe trying for another child would bring healing to both of them, but with Robin's continued efforts to isolate herself, he was not sure how to even approach the subject of intimacy. Sometimes he wondered if she blamed him. Sometimes she wondered the same about him. Neither spoke it aloud.

By April, Matt felt more optimistic. His grief had begun to ease. He had moments of hope again. Even so, he still slept on the futon in the basement most nights. On the rare occasions he had gone upstairs, Robin left the master bedroom and slept in another part of the house.

The spring rains began. Robin lay in bed, staring out at the gray sky. Her eyes were still swollen and sore from hours of crying. She knew she would not eat today either. Her stomach was weak, and the thought of food made her nauseated. She did not care if she ever ate again. Sometimes she still felt the phantom weight of Bryan in her arms, and the memory broke her open every time.

Olivia sat on her bedroom floor, playing with her dolls before whispering a short prayer. She missed Robin. She missed the closeness they used to have.

Taking a risk, Olivia stood and walked to the master bedroom. The door was cracked, so she knocked lightly and stepped inside. She came around to Robin's side of the bed and sat down. She glanced over her shoulder and saw Robin's eyes open.

Without prompting, Olivia began. "You taught me everything you could about helping people. You talked to me about what happens when we die, and how we can help the ones who are left behind. So, I want to help you."

Robin's eyes met Olivia's.

"You told me about spirit guides, and how each one has a job," Olivia continued. "You said there is a guide that makes us happy when we are sad. So why isn't yours doing that? It kind of seems like your guide might be really tired."

A faint smile tugged at Robin's lips. Olivia's honesty and innocence amused her in a way nothing else had in months.

"I know you are sad about Bryan," Olivia said softly, "but the guides tell me he is okay and that he is in the light. That is exactly where he is supposed to be." She twisted her fingers in her lap, suddenly shy. "I don't have to wonder if what you taught me is true now. I can feel it. I see people all the time. They stand there waiting for me. They need help, so I try to help them. And I think you need help too. I don't think I am supposed to help just dead people. I think I can help living people too. At least... I hope so."

Tears brimmed in Robin's bloodshot eyes. She lifted a thin, trembling hand and touched Olivia's cheek. "You are a very special girl, Olly. Do you know that?"

"I didn't know how special I was until Dad found you," she said. "He loves you more than anything. I love you. I wish you had been my real mom, but I am still glad you are here." She hesitated, then added bravely, "Baby Bryan is safe. My guides say he has been on Earth lots of times before. He was needed somewhere else this time."

Robin's eyes drifted toward the window. Tears pooled onto the sheets. "But I miss him," she whispered.

"You don't have to miss him," Olivia said gently. "His spirit watches you all the time. That is what you taught me. And it is true. He doesn't want you to be sad."

A faint spark of life flickered in Robin's eyes.

"Just listen," Olivia whispered. "Don't you hear it?"

The still, small voice Robin had come to rely on whispered again. She nodded as tears continued to fall.

"Peace," Olivia whispered. "They say peace."

She placed her palm on Robin's cheek. A sense of tranquility settled over Robin like a warm blanket. The heaviness began to loosen its grip. Something powerful, something healing, wrapped around her, and for the first time since Bryan's death, the unbearable weight began to lift.

"It's joy," Olivia said with a radiant smile. "Can you feel it?"

Robin sat up and took Olivia's hand. "Yes, Olly. I feel it."

Olivia nodded. "It's wonderful. But now you need to talk to Daddy. He is really worried about you."

Robin nodded. "I need a shower first. Then I will go downstairs."

They hugged tightly.

"We've missed you," Olivia whispered before walking downstairs.

A miracle. That was the only way Robin could explain it. She felt renewal. Peace.

She dressed in blue sweats and a graphic t-shirt, then walked downstairs into the living room. Matt sat on the couch watching television. She sank down beside him. He muted the screen immediately, turning toward her with disbelief and relief in his face.

"Well, there is something I've missed," he said.

Her lips curved into a shy smile. "I'm sorry, Matt," she murmured, fidgeting with her hand.

"You do not need to apologize," he said gently. "I was just scared for you. For us."

"I've been a zombie. The guilt consumed me. The anger. Olly… she rescued me. She reminded me that healing comes from inside me. Wanting to be happy does not mean I miss Bryan any less."

Matt slid closer and wrapped an arm around her, pulling her into an embrace. She had missed the warmth of him, the comfort of his scent. It felt wonderful to be close again.

"We have to find an answer for this house," Robin said quietly. "We cannot live like this."

He nodded. "I believe you were pushed down the stairs."

Robin stared at him in shock. "Really?"

"Yes. There were large handprints on your back. The doctor questioned me for hours. It made no sense. I am thankful they didn't arrest me."

"Matt... I am so sorry."

He shook his head. "I want to sell the house. I want out. Every night I sleep down there, I think about packing us up and never coming back."

"Are you sure?"

"Yes. I have thought a lot about it since we lost Bryan. I don't want to live like this anymore. You have been tortured and nearly killed. I cannot keep watching it. I think we have done everything we can."

"I don't think we have done everything we can yet," she said gently.

"What do you mean?"

"I still have the contact information for the Midwest Ghost Hunters. Why don't we call them?"

"Are you serious?" His voice lifted with disbelief and fear.

"It is the last thing we haven't tried."

He rubbed his forehead. "I hate that this is where we are, but I don't know what else to do. "He exhaled. "Alright. If that doesn't work, we'll sell the place."

A moment passed.

"But before we do anything," he said softly, "I want us to take a trip. We need to get away for a while. I owe you a honeymoon anyway. When we get back, we'll deal with everything."

49

After a honeymoon cruise in the Gulf, Robin and Matt returned home determined to resolve whatever was happening at Pikeview. Robin reached out to the Midwest Ghost Hunters and spoke with Jennifer Zanderheart, the founder of the group. Jennifer agreed to come to the home with her team for a consultation.

At seven o'clock on Wednesday evening, a caravan of vans and cars made its way up the lane. Robin and Matt waited at the west entrance. Despite Matt's protests, Olivia insisted on being home for the visit.

Inside, Jennifer introduced her team. Her older sister, Gabbie Zanderheart, and Alice Vanhoose had formed the group ten years earlier. What began as a hobby gradually shifted into scientific investigation as technology advanced.

Gabbie was a trance-medium, short in stature with red hair, glasses, and a peaceful presence. Alice, a petite brunette with sharp eyes, carried an intensity that filled the room. Jennifer's husband, Jacob Zanderheart, and Rodney Peaking followed. They served as technical specialists.

Jacob, six-foot-five with curly brown hair and a full beard, had married Jennifer right out of high school. Both had developed an interest in the paranormal when they were young. Their day jobs were in customer service and construction, respectively.

Rodney was Jacob's best friend. He was slightly shorter and stockier, with dirty-blonde hair and a pleasant smile. He and Jacob had worked on numerous construction sites together. Jacob's love of electronics connected him with Rodney, and over time Rodney became part of the team. His analytical skills were a valuable asset.

Once everyone sat around the dining table, Jennifer explained that as a trance-medium, Gabbie often saw things through the eyes of the dead. She sometimes experienced their emotions and sensations and could communicate with them after death. Alice specialized in demonology and was well-read and published in the field, which eased some of Matt's skepticism.

Robin and Matt explained everything they knew about the history of Pikeview Manor. They shared the research, the tragic deaths, the patterns between families, and the cemetery in the woods. They passed around the photographs Matt had taken during their exploration.

To Matt's surprise, the team simply listened and took notes. No one seemed judgmental. He realized they had likely seen worse situations than the one he and Robin were living in.

While the adults talked, Olivia sat at the end of the table working on a crossword puzzle. Gabbie kept glancing her way until finally she leaned slightly toward her.

"Hi there," she said.

"Hello," Olivia replied.

Gabbie turned her attention back to Matt. "Your daughter is gifted, Dr. Gregory. She sees things and hears things. The trauma she suffered opened her gifts. She is welcomed in the spirit world and is gaining a reputation on the other side. She is very special."

Matt's uncertainty showed. He hadn't expected a stranger to know anything about Olivia.

Jennifer shifted the conversation. "From what you've told me, the house was blessed, but things didn't improve. They actually seem to have gotten worse."

The others nodded.

"There appear to be three spirits who come and go often," she continued. "There is also a dark presence here, and right now it is overpowering everything. Because of your recent loss, both of you are vulnerable. The entity is dangerous."

"You two have argued more than usual the last few years," Alice said. "That is out of character for both of you. You are usually calm and communicative, but the energy here has stirred conflict."

Matt and Robin acknowledged the truth in her observation.

"So here is the plan," Jennifer said. "Tomorrow night we will set up equipment while you are out of the house. We will take baseline readings and see if we can document any unusual activity. That will help us determine what needs to happen next."

They agreed.

Gabbie spoke next. "Today we want to do a walkthrough. Rodney and Jacob will stay here with you, Matt."

Alice looked at Robin and Olivia. "We would like the two of you to come with us. Much of the anger seems directed at Robin. With Olivia's abilities, her presence may help us understand what is happening."

Matt immediately tensed. "I don't know if I am comfortable with that."

"She will be safe," Jennifer assured him.

Robin touched his hand. "I will not let anything happen to her."

He nodded, still uneasy.

The group walked to the parlor first. No one sensed anything unusual. In the kitchen, Gabbie suddenly stopped.

"We need to go to the basement," she said.

Robin led them down the stairs. In the middle of the basement, Gabbie began sketching quickly as she moved.

"What do you see?" Alice asked.

Gabbie handed her the pad. Alice's expression shifted, and she handed it to Robin.

Robin felt her stomach twist. The image was from her dreams. A man hung from a rafter in the basement.

"I dreamed this," she whispered. "This is the butcher. His real name…"

"Is Sims," Gabbie said.

Robin stared at her in disbelief. "Yes. Michael Sims."

They finished exploring the basement and moved upstairs. At the top of the second-floor landing, Jennifer suddenly froze.

"Good God, do you smell that?"

Alice inhaled lightly. "Something rotting. Decay."

Robin smelled nothing.

Alice looked at Robin and Olivia. "Go downstairs."

They returned to the dining room. Olivia resumed her crossword while Robin sat nervously, hands clasped.

After twenty minutes, the women reentered.

"You do have a demon," Alice said.

Jennifer nodded. "And it has been here a long time."

"Sims practiced occult rituals," Gabbie added. "Dark arts. He created the perfect environment for something demonic to take hold."

Alice's expression softened. "This is what pushed you down the stairs when you miscarried."

Jennifer leaned forward. "We can cleanse the property, but first the house needs an exorcism."

Matt shook his head. "We are not Catholic."

"You do not have to be," Jennifer said. "We can bring in a pastor or a tribal spiritual leader. It depends on your beliefs."

Gabbie studied Robin. "You were very religious once."

"Yes," Robin said. "I am a spiritualist now."

Matt looked overwhelmed. Alice reassured him. "You do not need to understand everything for the ritual to work."

Matt asked, "Which is better?"

Jennifer answered, "Given the strength of what is in this house, I recommend a pastor or priest."

Robin asked the group for a moment alone and sent Olivia to show them to the porch.

Matt rubbed his forehead. "I do not understand any of this. I feel lost."

"I understand enough to know Jennifer is right," Robin said. "I trust a pastor for something this strong. I have seen Richard handle things like this before."

"I just want this to end," Matt said. "If something wants to hurt you, I cannot live here."

They invited the investigators back inside.

"We have decided on an exorcism with a pastor," Robin said.

Jennifer nodded. "I will contact someone. Meanwhile, we will take readings, collect data, and document everything we can."

Jacob finally spoke. "We will set up video cameras."

Matt took Robin's hand. "I believe in what I can measure. I have tried to reason all of this away. But I have watched you and Olivia suffer while I pretended none of it was real."

Jennifer nodded. "Dr. Gregory, the paranormal exists whether you believe it or not. Our work follows scientific method and is well-documented."

Alice said, "We have recorded shadow people. We have witnessed exorcisms."

Gabbie added, "We have all seen things most people would call fiction."

Alice looked directly at Matt. "The presence in this house is one of the strongest I have encountered. It wants your wife dead. If you stay here long enough, it will make it happen. It will look like an accident, but it will not be accidental."

Gabbie continued, "It hates her. It could be a fire or another fall. The goal is the same."

Matt's voice was quiet. "Why Robin?"

"Her faith," Gabbie said.

Jennifer nodded. "She carries light. Darkness reacts violently to that."

Alice added, "She understands the spirit world and tries to walk honorably. That makes her a threat."

Jennifer looked at Matt. "No offense, Dr. Gregory, but you are not a threat. You don't believe."

Matt swallowed. "Why has Olivia been spared?"

"She is protected by spirits here and on the other side," Jennifer said. "Robin confronted the demon directly. That is why the entity targets her. Her strength challenges it. We are going to help you restore light to this house."

50

On Sunday night, while the paranormal team gathered data, Matt and Robin took Cookie and stayed with Terri and Wendy. Olivia stayed with the O'Bryans. Robin replayed everything the team had told her. For the first time, it felt like an answer might finally be within reach.

Robin, Matt, Olivia, and Cookie returned to Pikeview Manor Monday morning. Robin and Matt decided to work from home while Olivia went to school.

When Robin walked into the study, she heard Matt typing quickly. She leaned over him, wrapped her arms around his shoulders, kissed the side of his head, and stepped out.

Matt continued working. A faint drop in temperature brushed the back of his neck, subtle enough that he might have ignored it on any other day. He turned, expecting to see Cookie or Robin again, but instead noticed a shifting shadow trailing quietly behind her. Something about the movement made his chest tighten.

"Robin."

He rushed into the hallway. Robin had already turned toward him, and she walked directly into a dense, murky shape that seemed to absorb the light around it. Her breath caught instantly. She reached for her throat as if something had closed around it. Cookie barked from behind Matt but stayed low, ears flat, unwilling to come closer.

Matt ran to Robin and grabbed her shoulders. He tried pulling her back, unsure of what he was fighting against. Her face reddened as she struggled for air. He pulled harder, panic rising with every second she couldn't breathe.

"Let go of her!" he shouted into the empty hallway.

He felt nothing holding her except the rigid tension in her body. His pulse hammered as he tried again, desperate for any sign she could breathe.

Movement caught his attention. Olivia stood in her bedroom doorway, her fists tight at her sides. Her eyes were fixed on the space around Robin, narrowed in a way that made Matt stop for half a second.

"I see you," she whispered.

A low vibration moved through the air, hardly more than a rumble, but enough to raise the hairs on Matt's arms.

"Dear Jesus, help me," Matt said under his breath, not knowing what else to do.

The pressure released suddenly. Robin collapsed to her knees, coughing and gasping as she tried to draw air back into her lungs. The shadow dissolved in the space around them, disappearing as quietly as it had formed.

Matt dropped with her and pulled her into his arms. "Are you okay?"

She nodded between coughs, her voice too strained to speak yet.

Matt looked toward Olivia. "Go downstairs and get a glass of water."

Olivia turned and ran down the steps.

Robin took several shaky breaths, trying to steady herself.

"I don't understand this," Matt said quietly. His hands were trembling. "They're right. If we stay here, this thing is going to kill you."

"I'll be okay," Robin whispered, her voice uneven. "We're closer to a solution than we've ever been."

Later that day, once the house felt calm again, Robin sat in the parlor working on budget items. Matt paused in the doorway until she motioned for him to come in.

He took a seat across from her. The bruising on her neck had deepened into a dark, uneven pattern that made his stomach twist. "How are you going to cover that?"

"I have scarves," she said, keeping her attention on the laptop.

"Robin," Matt said as he settled into the wingback chair, "if this doesn't work... if the investigators can't stop this... we have to move. I'm not staying here at the risk of losing you."

Robin removed her reading glasses and looked directly at him. The strain on his face told her everything she needed to know. His fear wasn't exaggerated. It was real.

"I've been looking at places in town," he continued. "If we sell Pikeview, we won't lose everything, but it will set us back for a while."

"I understand." She folded her hands in her lap.

"I bought this house because it felt like something we could build together," he said. "I still remember when I brought you here the first time."

Robin exhaled. "Leaving wasn't hard in the beginning. I wasn't attached yet. But now it feels like walking away would mean giving up on everything we've tried to make here. And I know how out of control this has become."

"Exactly. I love this house. I love what we've done here. But I love you more. I can't keep watching this happen to you."

Robin stood and moved to the chair beside him. She rested her hand on his.

"Wherever you go, I go," she said softly. "That's how it's always been."

"I don't want this to be the end," he admitted.

"It's not the end," she said. "It's just a turn in the road."

51

Jennifer called a meeting at Pikeview to go over the findings from their night in the home. Robin and Matt sat at the dining room table with her, tension quietly settled between them. One look at Jennifer's expression told them the news was not good. Matt rested his hand over Robin's, grounding her.

Jennifer opened her laptop. "Before we start, I want you both to know that everything I'm going to show you was documented with standard equipment. Nothing here is altered. If you need to pause or step out, just tell me."

Robin and Matt exchanged a look of quiet understanding. They knew the footage would not be easy.

"Ready?" Jennifer asked.

They nodded.

The first video showed the upstairs hallway. The static camera had been positioned to cover several doorways. The study light flickered in short, irregular bursts. A moment later, heavy footsteps moved toward the camera. They weren't exaggerated or loud, but rhythmic and steady, like someone walking quickly with purpose.

A series of muted bangs came from the study, enough to make the hallway light flicker again.

Matt exhaled slowly. "That didn't happen when we were upstairs."

"No. This was during the quietest part of the night," Jennifer said. "Activity tends to increase when there's no human movement."

A dark shape appeared in the study doorway. It held the outline of a person but blurred around the edges, as if partly obscured. It hovered, then withdrew into the room.

Jennifer paused briefly before moving forward, giving them a moment to absorb what they had seen.

The next clip showed the study. The lights flickered again. The desk chair slid several inches on its casters before tipping onto its side. A picture frame rattled on the wall, then fell and shattered on the floor.

The shadow appeared in the doorway again. As it drifted closer, the footage distorted. Instead of revealing a face or form, the image scattered into static, then went completely black, as though the camera sensor had been overwhelmed.

"This kind of interference happens when the EM field spikes beyond what the camera can handle," Jennifer said quietly. "We recorded EMF levels in the study that were ten times the baseline readings."

Matt's shoulders stiffened. He didn't speak.

Jennifer clicked again. The basement came into view. A faint, transparent figure repeated the same pacing pattern near the laundry table. He faded in and out, but never approached the camera, never interacted.

"We also recorded a barometric pressure drop of 0.12 within a ten-second window," Jennifer said. "That's significant."

Next came footage of the east field. Pale orbs drifted across the screen, moving in consistent paths rather than random patterns.

Matt leaned closer. "So these aren't insects?"

"No. We compared this footage to infrared and checked frames for wing patterns," Jennifer said. "These maintain their shape through the entire sequence. They also move independently of air currents."

She switched to a series of graphs. "These are temperature and EMF readings throughout the house. Baseline is on the left. The right shows rapid drops of ten to fifteen degrees in specific rooms. There's no airflow source, no HVAC shifts, nothing natural to account for it."

Robin and Matt nodded, following along intently.

"What you're about to hear is EVP audio," Jennifer said. "These are electronic voice phenomena. We ask questions and let digital recorders pick up frequencies below human hearing. Later we run them through a spectral analysis program to isolate patterns."

She played the next clip. Gabbie stood in the basement holding a digital recorder and an EMF meter.

"What is your name?" she asked.

The voice software beneath the screen showed spikes before a faint, static-laced whisper formed something close to the word "Sims."

"Did she hear that?" Matt asked quietly.

"No. That's why we rely on analysis afterward."

On video, Gabbie continued. "Why are you here?"

A long pause. Then the spectral monitor pulsed.

"My house," the distorted voice murmured.

"Do you want to leave?" she asked.

After several seconds, another quiet reply came. "No."

Alice stepped forward. "Can we help you?"

Silence. The EMF meter in Gabbie's hand spiked from 0.1 to 2.4.

Gabbie rubbed her arms slightly. "He's close. Right behind me."
The video captured nothing but stillness.

Jennifer moved on.

Olivia's room appeared on the screen.

"Who are you?" Gabbie asked.

A soft but clear voice replied, "Emma."

Alice's eyebrows lifted. "That was audible."

"Yes," Gabbie said. "Rare, but it happens."

An orb crossed the camera. The EVP monitor spiked again.

A faint whisper followed: "I'm fine."

Jennifer switched to another audio recording. "This was taken in your study."

Her voice played back. "Who are you?"

Silence.

"What do you want?"

The monitor flickered. A low, strained sound came through, as if the recorder had picked up a breath against the microphone.

Slowly, a fragmented word formed: something close to "souls," though distorted enough to leave room for interpretation.

Matt straightened, jaw tight. Robin's fingers curled together, knuckles pale.

Jennifer's voice played again. "Can we help you?"

The reply this time was sharper, clearer, as if spoken directly into the recorder.

"Get out."

Robin and Matt exchanged a long, heavy look.

"So what happens next?" Matt asked quietly.

Jennifer folded her hands. "Based on all the data, you need a minister, pastor, or priest to perform a cleansing and exorcism. The activity here is intelligent and territorial. If the ritual doesn't resolve it, you may need to leave the home permanently."

Robin steadied her breathing. "What started all of this?"

"My belief is that construction disturbed dormant energy in the house," Jennifer said. "Spirits become active when foundations shift or old rooms are opened. Sims is residual and territorial, not malicious. The woman you've seen may be in a looping state or trying to communicate. Emma is fully aware and chooses not to cross over. The demonic presence is the greatest concern. It latches onto instability and unresolved trauma."

She hesitated before continuing. "Olivia's sensitivity is unlike most I've seen. Children with her level of intuition often act as mediators between energies. If you consent, we would like her to participate."

Matt shook his head almost instinctively. "She's a child."

"I understand," Jennifer said calmly. "But she has already interacted with these entities without prompting. That suggests they see her whether she's involved or not."

Robin spoke softly. "She's ready. She's stronger than we think."

Matt didn't answer. He stared at the table, overwhelmed.

"Just think it over," Jennifer said gently.

Robin asked, "How soon can the exorcism be done?"

"I'll call the pastor as soon as I leave," Jennifer replied. "The sooner, the better. Until then, I don't think this house is fully safe."

52

As Robin sat in her office at work, she tried to keep her mind on the files spread across her desk, but her thoughts drifted constantly. She was staying at a hotel while Matt and Olivia remained in the house, waiting on Jennifer to line up a pastor for the exorcism. Everyone agreed Robin shouldn't return until it was done, though the separation gnawed at her.

She reread the same paragraph of a report three times. The department had been running on autopilot ever since things worsened at Pikeview. She worried the administration might be noticing her slip but lingering on that wouldn't help. She straightened a stack of files and forced herself to keep going.

A quiet knock at her door made her jump. She looked up to see Matt standing there, hands shoved in his pockets, looking unsure if he should come in.

"Hey," she said, surprised. "What are you doing here?"

"I figured you might want lunch." He stepped inside, closing the door gently. "Feels like I haven't really seen you in days."

She blinked. "How'd you get off work?"

"I took a little time." His shrug was casual, but something about it made her think it wasn't easy for him to do.

"I just need to sign off on a few files. Then we can go," she said.

He sat on the worn leather couch across from her desk. For a moment, he simply watched her with quiet seriousness.

"Robin," he said softly.

She looked up from her paperwork.

"I know things have been... a lot. The house. Everything you've told me about your childhood. Bryan." He rubbed the back of his neck, searching for words. "I just wanted you to know I see how hard you're trying. Even when you don't feel like yourself."

Robin wasn't prepared for how much she needed to hear that. Something tightened in her chest, and she looked away, embarrassed by the warmth rising in her cheeks.

He gave a faint smile. "Haven't seen you blush in a while."

She shook her head lightly. "You always know how to throw me off."

"Well," he said, "I mean it."

She stood and crossed the office, sitting beside him. "In spite of everything I've been through, it was still easy to fall in love with you," she said quietly. "Maybe too easy."

He kissed her forehead. "Come on. Let's get some food before you decide to keep working instead."

Two weeks passed with only a few short updates from Jennifer saying she was still trying to secure a pastor. The delay wore Robin thin. She was tired of living out of a suitcase, tired of feeling like a visitor in her own life.

Finally, she decided to do something herself.

She went to the local metaphysical shop for sage, then to the grocery store for sea salt. She knew how to perform a cleansing. The only question was whether Matt would agree to let Olivia help.

Taking a breath, she walked down the basement stairs.

Matt was punching the leather bag hanging from a floor joist. Sweat streaked down his face. His tank top clung to his back. The sound of each hit echoed through the room; he wasn't just exercising. He was letting out fear.

"Hey," she said cautiously.

He stopped and grabbed the bag. "Hey." His voice was worn. He walked to the laundry table and took a long drink of water.

"I need to ask you something," she said.

"Okay." He braced himself.

"I'm going to do a cleansing tomorrow. And… I want to include Olivia." She hesitated; she knew this wouldn't go over well. "She can communicate with the spirits. I can't. Together we can help Sims, the woman in the field, and Emma. I can't handle the demon, but I know we can help the others."

Matt shook his head. "Robin, she's a kid. And I'm barely holding it together with all of this."

"She's gifted," Robin said gently. "And ignoring it doesn't protect her. It just scares her more."

"What if something happens to her?" His voice cracked slightly. "You didn't see her face the last time that thing showed up. She's still just a little girl."

Robin stepped closer and took his hand. "Nothing will happen to her. I love her too. And you'll be with us. If anything feels off, we stop."

"The whole thing feels off," he muttered.

"I've done cleansings before. I know what I'm doing. And I can't stay in that hotel much longer. I need to try something." She swallowed. "Do you trust me?"

A long moment passed before he finally nodded. "Yeah. Of course I do."

"Then let us try."

He gave a reluctant nod.

The next afternoon, when Olivia got home from school, Robin and Matt sat on the couch while she ate a snack at the coffee table. Robin took a breath to start explaining, but before she could say anything, Olivia turned and looked at her.

"I kinda already know," she said, brushing crumbs off her fingers.

Matt frowned. "Know what?"

"That you need my help with the three ghosts."

His eyebrows rose. "How did you know that?"

"I just felt it." She shrugged and turned back toward the TV.

Robin and Matt exchanged a look.

"Olivia," Matt said gently, "are you okay helping?"

"I can talk to the nice ones," she said. "Not the scary one. I don't like him."

"We're not asking you to talk to him," Robin said.

"Good. Because nope."

Robin almost laughed despite the tension.

She went to the kitchen and pulled the sage, feather, and lighter from the paper bag.

"Open the windows," she called to Matt.

He did, though he watched everything with wary eyes.

Robin lit the sage, and the smoke curled softly through the room. She waved the feather, guiding the smoke.

"What does the sage do?" Matt asked.

"It helps clear energy," she said. "And the salt seals the doorways."

She looked at Olivia. "Can you call to them?"

Olivia nodded. "Emma's already here. She says she doesn't want to stay long. She's scared the demon will find her."

"She doesn't need to be afraid," Robin said softly.

Olivia turned toward the window. "Emma… go to the light. You'll be okay. I promise."

A quiet moment passed.

"She still doesn't want to go," Olivia said. Then she squinted, concentrating. "Oh. She sees her mom and dad. She's smiling."

Robin felt tears prickle her eyes.

"Go to them, Emma," Olivia said gently. "They've been waiting."

After a moment she turned back. "She says she'll miss us. But she's going."

"How'd you tell her that?" Matt asked.

Olivia tapped her temple. "In here." She paused. "She's gone now."

Robin swallowed and continued the cleansing. Olivia walked beside her, pausing when something shifted.

In the dining room, Olivia stopped. "The lady's here. She wants to leave too."

She pointed toward an empty corner. "That light's for you."

She nodded to someone they couldn't see. "I'll tell them."

"Tell us what?" Matt asked.

"She says she's sorry for scaring you. And Mr. Sims… he lied to her. She stayed to look for her baby, and the demon wouldn't let her go."

Robin steadied herself. "Where's Mr. Sims now?"

"He won't come to me."

Matt's brow furrowed. "Why not?"

"Then we go to him," Robin said.

They headed to the basement.

"Mr. Sims," Olivia called softly, "I can see you. I can help you if you let me."

Robin and Matt held still.

"He says he did too many bad things," Olivia murmured. "He thinks the light will punish him."

"He can't stay," Matt said, voice firm. "We don't want him here."

"He sees the light," Olivia said. "He's scared. He says he's sorry. He said the darkness changed him."

She drew in a breath. "Mr. Sims… you have to go. You can't stay here anymore."

A faint draft moved across the room.

"He's gone."

They walked the property line afterward, laying down salt and offering blessings. The air felt lighter, but not clear.

The human spirits were gone.

The demon was not.

And for the first time, Robin felt the truth of what Richard once said. The veil wasn't just thin.

It was breaking.

53

As Matt sat in his office at work, he typed a report for the board of directors, reading the same paragraph twice before realizing he had not absorbed a word of it. His patience was wearing thin. Since the cleansing, the house had been quiet, but the calm felt temporary, like a pause rather than an ending.

He thought about how wrong he had been. What had happened at Pikeview did not fit within any explanation he had relied on for most of his life. It was not something he could dismiss or rationalize away. There was more beyond the physical world. Admitting that did not bring him comfort. It brought responsibility.

His cell phone rang, startling him. He glanced at the screen. Jennifer.

"This is Dr. Gregory," he answered.

"Dr. Gregory, this is Jennifer with Midwest Ghost Hunters."

"I was starting to wonder if we would hear from you again," he said, unable to keep the edge from his voice.

"I understand," she replied calmly. "I did not want to involve anyone unless I was confident. I have spoken with a pastor I trust, and he has agreed to help."

Matt closed his eyes briefly. "When?"

"He can come tomorrow, if that works for you. With your permission, the team would like to document the session."

"That's fine," Matt said. "I just want this handled."

"We can also assist with crossing over any remaining spirits, if needed."

Matt explained that the human spirits had already been addressed. He told her about the cleansing and about Olivia's involvement. Jennifer sounded relieved.

After a moment, Matt agreed that Olivia could be present, as long as she stayed close to him.

When the call ended, Matt set his phone down and leaned back in his chair. His gaze drifted to the wall across from him, though he did not really see it. He thought about the house, about Robin, about Olivia.

Whatever was coming next could not be prepared for or explained away. He understood that now. All he could do was remain steady, stand where he was needed, and protect what mattered.

Tomorrow, he would face what he could no longer deny.

54

Jennifer and her team arrived the next afternoon at 4:30. They moved through the house quietly, setting up their equipment without conversation. There was no sense of performance, only preparation. When the pastor arrived, Jennifer explained that Dean Williams had spent many years in deliverance ministry. He was steady and deeply rooted in his faith. She trusted him.

Dean pulled into the drive and stepped out of his car. Matt met him outside, and they exchanged a firm handshake.

"You must be Dr. Gregory," Dean said.

"I am. Thank you for coming."

Inside, everyone gathered in the kitchen. Dean greeted Robin politely, shaking her hand.

"Mrs. Gregory."

"Hello," she replied.

"If you don't mind, I'd like to walk through the house for a few minutes," he said.

"Of course."

When Dean returned, his expression was thoughtful rather than alarmed.

"Let's begin in the parlor," he said.

They followed him down the hallway.

"This your workspace?" he asked Robin.

"Yes."

He nodded slowly. "This house has carried fear. But fear does not have authority here."

He asked them to pray.

Robin reached for Matt's hand. He held it tightly, grounding himself in the familiar weight of her fingers. As Dean prayed aloud, Matt found himself whispering words he did not fully understand. They did not come from certainty or knowledge. They came from surrender.

The room grew quiet. Not empty, but dense, as if the air itself had drawn inward.

Olivia stood close to Matt, holding his other hand. Her lips moved silently. Her face was intent in a way that was no longer childlike.

Robin spoke softly. "Creator of this world and the next, please bring peace to this home."

Her breath caught. Panic surged through her without warning, sharp and physical. She bent forward, gasping, one hand pressed to her chest as if something long buried had been pulled loose.

Matt moved toward her immediately.

"Just breathe," Dean said calmly.

Robin struggled for air, her body reacting before her thoughts could catch up. Grief, fear, memory all folded into the same familiar response. She understood then that belief did not shield her from pain. It simply asked her to endure it again.

"I'm okay," she said finally, though her voice trembled.

Dean nodded. "Sometimes peace comes through release."

They moved upstairs to the study. The group formed a loose circle. Dean stood at the center and began to pray again, his voice low and steady.

"Whatever has lingered here no longer has permission to remain. This house belongs to the living."

As the final words left his mouth, a deep sound moved through the house. Not a crash. Not a bang. A long, settling groan that traveled from the upper floors down into the floor beneath their feet, like a structure releasing years of strain all at once.

Everyone froze.

Matt felt it through the soles of his shoes.

The lights flickered once, then went dark.

Robin gasped. Matt's heart slammed into his ribs as he tightened his grip on her and reached instinctively for Olivia, already moving her closer to his side.

Then the lights snapped back on.

The house was still.

Before anyone could speak, Olivia lifted her head.

"It's gone," she said.

Her voice was calm. Certain.

Dean fell silent. He did not speak right away.

When he finally did, his voice was quieter than before. "It's done."

The authority in his words landed heavier than anything he had said all afternoon.

The tension in the room began to ease. Not suddenly. Gradually. Like something withdrawing rather than being forced out.

When the silence settled, it felt altered. Not triumphant. Not relieved. Simply changed.

In that stillness, Matt understood something with absolute clarity. The world he had trusted to be orderly and explainable had split open. What lay beyond it was real, and knowing that came with responsibility. He would never be able to unknow it. He would spend the rest of his life deciding when to speak and when to remain silent.

Robin stared at the floor, aware of the familiar weight settling back onto her shoulders. This was not an ending. It was another layer added to a life already shaped by loss and survival. She would carry it, as she always had, because someone had to.

Olivia did not relax. While the adults stood quietly, she remained still, her gaze fixed on the far corner of the room. She felt the shift more than she understood it. Something had changed, and no one had words for it. She knew, in the simple way children know things, that this awareness would set her apart. That it already had.

Jennifer and her team packed up without comment. Dean offered his thanks and left without ceremony.

Matt helped Robin to her feet and drew both her and Olivia into his arms. He held them there, listening to the house.

It sounded the same.

It felt different.

"It's over," he said softly.

But even as he said it, he knew the truth.

What had ended was the danger they could name. What remained would shape them in ways they could not yet see.

And they would move forward carrying it. Together. Silently.

Epilogue

What had once felt like endless torment came to a stop. Not cleanly. Not completely. But enough for life to move forward.

Robin and Matt had endured more than either of them would have chosen. They did not come through it untouched, but they came through it together. Matt's tentative steps toward faith settled into something quieter and heavier. He believed fully now, but he did not speak of it often. He had learned that some truths were not meant to be passed around. They were meant to be carried.

Robin came home. The house felt different. Not healed. Not sacred. Simply livable. She returned to work, to family, to the small routines that grounded her. Faith had never promised her safety. It had only ever asked her to endure, and she did.

Olivia went back to school. Back to friends. Back to the ordinary rhythms of childhood. Her gift did not disappear. It surfaced in quiet moments she did not talk about. She noticed things others missed. She watched longer. Listened harder. No one asked her to explain, and she did not try. Some kinds of knowing came with distance, and she was learning that early.

Time passed.

Robin became pregnant again and gave birth to a healthy baby boy, David Thomas Gregory. Years later, she stood in front of the mirror in their master bedroom, one hand resting on her pregnant belly. In just three weeks, they would welcome a baby girl. The name they had chosen was Hope Inez Gregory. Hope, because they needed it. Inez, for Robin's grandmother.

Robin tried to focus on getting ready, but her thoughts drifted.

Matt walked in. "Let's go. We're running late."

"I'm almost ready," she said, fastening her earrings.

"Olivia's already in the car, and David's tearing up the downstairs like a wild man." From outside, the car horn blared. "And now Olivia's honking like she's losing her mind. Can you hear that?"

Robin smiled. "You'd think this was her first awards banquet."

"Well, it's her first county academic achievement award," Matt said. "She's worked hard for it."

"I know. I got her something special." Robin nodded toward the dresser. "Top drawer."

Matt opened the small black box and lifted out the charm bracelet. A tiny ghost charm hung from the chain. He smiled. "She'll love this."

Robin slipped on her black heels. "I think I'm ready."

Matt stepped closer, resting his hand on her belly before kissing her cheek. "I love you," he said softly. "All of you."

He headed down the stairs while Robin followed more slowly, stopping at the kitchen door. She looked out at her family waiting in the car. Olivia leaned across the front seat, arm hanging out the window. David bounced beside her, full of noise and motion.

They looked like any other family in a hurry.

And in many ways, they were.

Life had resumed. Laughter filled the space where fear once lived. Schedules mattered again. Small annoyances returned. The house held.

But the past had not vanished. It followed them quietly, like a small red wagon trailing behind, its weight felt even when no one looked back. They did not talk about it. They did not need to. It shaped how they loved, how they protected one another, how they chose silence when words would cost too much.

What had ended was the danger they could name. What remained was the knowing they would carry.

And they went on living anyway.

ABOUT THE AUTHOR

Tracee Ford, known as the "Smart Mouth Writer," has been telling stories her whole life. She is an award-winning novelist whose work explores the intersection of love, belief, and the unseen forces that shape human lives.

Her debut novel, *The Fine Line*, received a Five Star Reader's Favorite Award. Her second novel, *Idolum*, was also honored by Reader's Favorite and nominated by the Paranormal Romance Guild for Best Romantic Suspense. *Through Glass Darkly* later earned first place for Best Paranormal Romance (General), and the *Between Worlds* series received additional recognition from the Paranormal Romance Guild.

Beyond fiction, Tracee has walked many creative paths as a playwright, director, and puppeteer. Her lifelong interest in the paranormal, paired with lived experience, informs her exploration of trauma, belief, and the quiet moments where ordinary life brushes up against something more.

www.ingramcontent.com/pod-product-compliance
Lightning Source LLC
Chambersburg PA
CBHW062135170626
46813CB00002B/707